"Sup

The

beside In

"I wo

must not   Rosamund.

. . . I am s   erstand.

"I will understand," the Viscount replied, "if you will say good-night to me."

Ina looked at him in surprise.

"What I am asking, Ina, is that you should let me kiss you good-night!"

With a little cry she pushed him away, saying:

"That is . . . something you should not . . . ask me!"

The Viscount caught her hand.

"But I have asked you," he said, "and I feel quite certain that I would not be the first man to kiss you . . ."

A Camfield Novel of Love by Barbara Cartland

"Barbara Cartland's novels are all distinguished by their intelligence, good sense, and good nature . . ."
—ROMANTIC TIMES

"Who could give better advice on how to keep your romance going strong than the world's most famous romance novelist, Barbara Cartland?"
—THE STAR

Camfield Place,
Hatfield
Hertfordshire,
England

Dearest Reader,

Camfield Novels of Love mark a very exciting era of my books with Jove. They have already published nearly two hundred of my titles since they became my first publisher in America, and now all my original paperback romances in the future will be published exclusively by them.

As you already know, Camfield Place in Hertfordshire is my home, which originally existed in 1275, but was rebuilt in 1867 by the grandfather of Beatrix Potter.

It was here in this lovely house, with the best view in the county, that she wrote *The Tale of Peter Rabbit*. Mr. McGregor's garden is exactly as she described it. The door in the wall that the fat little rabbit could not squeeze underneath and the goldfish pool where the white cat sat twitching its tail are still there.

I had Camfield Place blessed when I came here in 1950 and was so happy with my husband until he died, and now with my children and grandchildren, that I know the atmosphere is filled with love and we have all been very lucky.

It is easy here to write of love and I know you will enjoy the Camfield Novels of Love. Their plots are definitely exciting and the covers very romantic. They come to you, like all my books, with love.

Bless you,

A New Camfield Novel of Love by

BARBARA CARTLAND

Wanted - A Wedding Ring

JOVE BOOKS, NEW YORK

WANTED—A WEDDING RING

A Jove Book / published by arrangement with
the author

PRINTING HISTORY
Jove edition / August 1987

ISBN: 0-515-09111-1

Jove Books are published by The Berkley Publishing Group,
200 Madison Avenue, New York, New York 10016.
The name "JOVE" and the "J" logo
are trademarks belonging to Jove Publications, Inc.

PRINTED IN THE UNITED STATES OF AMERICA

10 9 8 7 6 5 4 3 2 1

Author's Note

A wedding ring is the most valuable treasure a woman can possess.

The Gaiety Girls all longed to get married and some of them actually did marry into the peerage. Rosie Boote became the Marchioness of Hertford, and Sylvia Lilian Story the Countess of Poulett.

Women have valued their wedding rings since Anglo-Saxon times. The Ancient Egyptians and Greeks wore gold rings and poorer Egyptians wore rings of silver, bronze, glass, or pottery. In the Roman Empire gold rings were worn by freeborn Roman citizens, silver rings by freedmen, and iron rings by slaves.

In the second century after Christ, Christians adopted the custom of using gold betrothal rings, and in time this ring became the wedding ring in the modern manner.

Plain gold bands were often too austere for some of our ancestors. The wedding ring was often embellished with stones, clasped hands, and even sentimental inscriptions.

Engagement rings set with precious stones were introduced in the Middle Ages and diamond rings became popular and customary about 1800.

It was believed that a gold wedding ring had more magic than any other metal, but actually it was the roundness of the ring that was essential. The magic virtues of a perfect circle have been recognised since antiquity.

Because a wedding ring is regarded as a love amulet with magical properties, unmarried girls often use a gold wedding ring borrowed for an occasion, in those practices by which they hope to gain a husband. This may be good for the girls, but dangerous for the wives who lend their rings.

It is known to be bad luck to remove a wedding ring from the finger. Bad luck for a wife means losing her husband's love.

In America, the old-fashioned custom of giving a wedding ring to a man has been revived. In England, a well-born Englishman considers it common to wear any ring except a very small signet ring on his little finger.

It was an Egyptian priest dissecting human bodies who found "a very fine nerve proceeded from the fourth finger on the left hand to the human heart."

It was therefore understandable this finger should be honoured by first the betrothal ring, then the wedding ring. There is, however, no mention of this little nerve in *Gray's Anatomy of the Human Body,* the most famous of all textbooks of anatomy.

Wanted - A Wedding Ring

chapter one

1898

Rosie Rill opened the letters which had come by post.

There were two birthday-cards, each of them from women of her own age.

She looked at them with an expression of horror.

Fifty-six! It could not be possible that she, Rosie Rill, was fifty-six today.

In ten years she would be sixty-six, and to all intents and purposes ready for the grave!

With a feeling of irritation she flung the birthday-cards down on the floor.

She then sat back staring blindly in front of her, as if by some miracle she could put time back and be eighteen again.

How well she could remember her eighteenth birthday.

It was something she would never forget, as it was the day she had met Vivian for the first time.

Even now she could see him walking towards her

as she rode down the drive under the ancient oak trees and wondered who he could be.

He was the best-looking man she had ever seen.

She was much too ignorant of men to realise that he was over-dressed for the country and his clothes were smarter than what a real gentleman would have worn.

All she could see at that moment were his dark eyes looking at her with an expression of admiration.

It made her feel for the first time in her life that she had met a man.

As she neared him she had reined in her horse.

"Good-morning!" he said. "You must forgive me if I am trespassing, but I understand this is the estate of the Earl of Ormond and Staverley."

"That is right," Rosie said in her soft, young voice.

"I feel, because you are so beautiful," Vivian went on, "that you must be the Earl's daughter."

The compliment made her blush, and looking delightfully shy she answered:

"Yes . . . I am Lady Rosamund Ormond."

Thinking back, Rosie could still feel the thrill that ran through her after they had talked a little while.

Then Vivian said:

"I must see you again—you know that—and I do not think I can wait very long for that to happen!"

There had, in fact, been meetings every day, twice a day, sometimes three times a day.

It was not difficult for Rosie to escape from the Big House.

Now that she was grown up, there was no Governess to find fault with everything she did.

Both her mother and her father were very busy people.

It was the time of the year when they had house-parties for local events and the Countess took her duties as a hostess very seriously.

Being so pre-occupied in organising the house-maids and having consultations with the cook, she never noticed that her daughter looked more beautiful than usual.

Also she was continually riding away from the house.

"Where have you been?" Rosie's father would occasionally growl at her at dinnertime.

"Exercising the horses, Papa. You know we are short-handed in the stables."

"Good girl, I can trust you not to take them too far."

"Of course, Papa. I am very careful not to do that."

The horses actually spent most of the time tied up to a gate or a tree in the wood, or let loose if they were the ones who came when she called them.

They were quite content to do nothing while Rosie talked to Vivian.

She learnt a great deal about him, or rather, what he wanted her to know, when they met secretly.

Because it was so exciting, she loved every moment of it, thinking over what he had said at night until even the stars seemed to twinkle his name.

Vivian Vaughan!

Could any man be more romantic or look more like the hero of her dreams?

It was not until years later that she learned that his real name was Bill Barton, and that he came from a small village in the Midlands.

However, at the moment he was a god who had stepped down from Olympus.

Her whole being responded to his good looks and the romantic things he said to her.

"How can you be so perfect?" he asked. "I had no idea until I saw you riding down the drive that anybody could look so exquisite!"

She felt that everything he said came from one of the Plays of her imagination in which she played the lead and he was the hero.

"You have never heard of me?" he asked in astonishment. "Well, I suppose it is understandable. At the same time, I am very well known in London, although perhaps not in the Theatres that you attend."

Rosie dimpled at him.

"I have only been allowed to see Shakespeare, and to listen to Concerts. But now that I am grown up I am to be presented to the Queen. I hope when I am in London to go to the Theatres and perhaps I could see you."

"You are coming to London?"

She heard the note of gladness in his voice and thought her heart was singing in response.

"Papa is going to open the London house for me," she explained, "and I am to have a Ball, and of course a Reception for all my older relatives."

She paused, then she said:

"Do you think you will be able to come?"

Vivian Vaughan laughed.

"My dear, I am very honoured that you should think of it, but you must be aware that your mother would not consider me the right sort of friend for a débutante."

"Why not?"

"Because I am an actor, and actors, although they amuse those who live in the Social World, are not *persona grata* with the parents of beautiful young ladies like yourself."

Vivian had been well educated, Rosie learned later, because his father had been a School-Master.

That was another reason why he knew, as he termed it bitterly, "his place."

They went on meeting every day until it was time

4

for him to return to London.

He had come to the country because he had picked up a troublesome cough during the winter which had affected his voice.

"If you are going to take part in this new Show," he had been told, "you will have to stop croaking! Get out of London, walk in the clean fresh air of the country, and get rid of that 'frog in your throat.'"

A fellow actor had told Vivian how beautiful the countryside was in the north of Hertfordshire.

He had also recommended a small Inn, where the food was good and the beds soft.

Vivian had intended to stay a week but, because of Rosie he had extended his "rest" as he called it, to three weeks.

"How can I leave you?" he asked despairingly when there were only three days left before he must go back to London.

"Perhaps I shall be able to see you sometimes when we come to London," Rosie said in a very low voice.

Even as she spoke she knew it was very unlikely.

She would never be allowed to go out of the house alone as she was in the country.

She knew Vivian was right when he said that he would not be welcome as a guest in her father's house.

It was then he had kissed her.

Before that he had been too afraid of scaring her away, besides which he had now genuinely fallen in love.

He really did think that this beautiful, untouched, unspoilt girl was someone from another world.

It was only when he held her in his arms and felt the softness and innocence of her lips that he knew how much he wanted her.

He could not bear to lose her.

He pleaded, cajoled, and beguiled Rosie, until she, who was already in love with him, found it impossible to deny him anything he wanted.

"We will be married," Vivian said insistently, "and then there will be nothing your father can do about it!"

"But . . . supposing," Rosie said in a very low voice, "he is so . . . angry that he will not . . . accept you?"

"He will have to, if I am your husband," Vivian replied. "I will get a Special Licence and we will be married on our way to London. Not until we arrive there will we tell your father what has happened."

"How can I do such a . . . thing? How . . . can I?" Rosie had asked herself as she tossed about in the bed she had slept in ever since she had grown out of her cot.

At the same time, how could she give up Vivian, and how could she bear that he should go away and leave her?

She would never again see his handsome face, his eloquent eyes, or hear him saying such beautiful things to her again.

They made her feel as if he drew her heart from her body and made it his.

"I love him! I love him!" she said defiantly, and knew that nothing mattered in the world except Vivian.

It was easier than she expected to leave home.

Her father and mother had an appointment at the other end of the County on the day that Vivian was to return to London, and they had left very early in the morning.

As soon as they were gone, Rosie, who had already planned what she would do, told the housemaids to pack everything she had laid out for them.

"Where are you goin', M'Lady? 'Is Lordship

never says nothin' before he left 'bout your goin' away."

"I am being collected at eleven o'clock," Rosie replied.

She had waited until Vivian arrived for her in a Chaise he had hired from the nearby Livery Stables.

As he walked up to her, the two young footmen stared at him in astonishment.

They obeyed Lady Rosamund when she told them to put her trunks on the back of the Chaise and set her dressing-case down in the front near her feet.

"Good-bye, Bates," she said to the Butler.

"What'll I tell His Lordship when he comes back this evening, M'Lady?" Bates asked.

There was an expression on his old face that told Rosie he was worried about what was happening.

He was even suspicious that it was something too outrageous even to be contemplated.

"Tell Papa I will write to him from London," Rosie answered.

She got into the Chaise, the footmen put a rug over her knees, and Vivian whipped up the horses and drove them down the drive.

She realised he did not drive as well as her father did.

Then she told herself it was disloyal for her to be critical of somebody so wonderful and whom she loved so completely.

"How could I have been such a little fool?" Rosie asked herself now.

Yet she had been happy when she was first married to Vivian, perhaps happier than she had ever been in the whole of her life.

It was only when she had a letter from her father saying she had forfeited the right to be called his daughter and he never wished to hear from her again did she realise what she had done.

Her father's attitude was a surprise to Vivian also.

She soon realised he did not have enough money to keep her as well as himself in the style to which he had become accustomed.

"You will have to find something to do," he said.

She had looked at him in astonishment.

"Do you mean . . . work?"

"I mean you must earn some money. We are in debt, and I need a new suit."

Too late Rosie wished she had brought more clothes away with her when she had left home.

Because it was Springtime she had packed only her summer gowns and left behind her winter clothes.

Now she did not dare tell Vivian that her coat was not really warm enough for the months of frost and snow which lay ahead.

She thought he was looking at her in a strange way, then he said but not as if he was paying a compliment:

"You are very beautiful, Rosie, and you have a slim, perfect figure, which is very important."

"Important for what?"

"For what I want you to do."

"And what is . . . that?"

"Act, of course. If I am an actor, then naturally, you must be an actress."

She stared at him in sheer astonishment. Then she said:

"No, no! Of course not! How could I do something which would make me very shy and frightened? And it would shock and horrify Mama!"

"I hardly think your mother's feelings need concern us, one way or the other," Vivian said coldly, "unless, of course, she were willing to give us an allowance; something we both omitted to think about when you left home."

Rosie felt the tears come into her eyes.

She was well aware how bitterly Vivian resented her father's ostracism of her because she had married him.

"Good God!" he said furiously. "You would think I was a crook or a criminal from the way they have behaved towards you!"

"Are you . . . sorry that I . . . ran away with you?" Rosie asked in a broken little voice.

He put his arms around her as he said:

"No, of course not! You know I love you, darling, of course I do. At the same time, it is difficult being without money."

"Yes . . . I know."

"And having struggled and fought to get where I have in the Theatre, I can't give up now."

"I . . . I am sorry, dearest, I am sorry that my family is so . . . unkind."

It was something she was to repeat again and again, even when she was earning money and eventually making as much, if not more, than Vivian.

She had known then it was not only because he loved her for herself that he had persuaded her to run away with him.

He had also been attracted by the aura of her background and by the fact that she was Lady Rosamund Ormond and that her father was an Earl.

On one thing, however, she was determined, and nothing Vivian could say would move her: If she did go on the stage, she would allow 'every Tom, Dick, and Harry,' as her father would say, to look at her.

But at least she would not drag her brothers and sisters into the dust by using her own name.

"Do you not understand what an asset your name is?" Vivian had argued. "They will want to bill you as 'Lady Rosamund.' You would get extra money and undoubtedly more admirers than you would otherwise have."

"I do not want . . . admirers when I have . . . you,"

Rosie retorted, "and I will not use my title or Papa's name."

She did not know why she was so obstinate.

Something proud that had been born in her rebelled against letting what she knew was the "tinsel of the Theatre" besmirch her family.

Her family had been part of the history of England all down the centuries.

When she was living at home she had never thought much about the Family-Tree which hung in her father's Study.

Also, she had not been particularly impressed by the flags brought back by her ancestors from numerous battles.

She had actually thought the Picture Gallery, with its endless faces of Ormonds, was rather over-powering and exceedingly dull.

Yet she could not bear the condemnation which she would see in their eyes if they knew an Ormond was appearing on the stage.

It was the only point on which she opposed Vivian.

Finally he gave up and chose instead a different name for her.

"Very well," he said bitterly, "but if you want to be theatrical, then you had better have something catchy that the public will remember—'Rosie' instead of Rosamund—and . . ."

He paused before he finished:

"'Rill' instead of 'Ormond.' 'Rosie Rill!' How does that appeal to you?"

"It will do," Rosie had said dully.

She was very near to tears because he was mocking at her.

Then with one of his quick changes of mood he put his arms around her and kissed her.

"What does it matter what you are called," he said

fiercely, "as long as you remain as lovely as you are now? You will 'knock them into a cocked hat,' my darling, there is no doubt about that."

Strangely enough, for things seldom work out the way one expects, that was exactly what Rosie did.

At first she had a very small part in a play in which Vivian had the lead.

Eventually, although she had only a few lines to speak, the audience clapped as soon as she appeared, and her part was extended.

"You are a success, my lovely one," Vivian said.

Because he seemed proud and pleased, Rosie was happy too.

It was impossible to make him understand how frightened she had been when the moment came for her to walk in front of the footlights.

To know that hundreds of strange eyes were staring at her.

At first she was so frightened, her voice seemed to die in her throat, and all she wanted was to run away.

Then she told herself that all those people staring at her were of no importance.

The only thing that mattered was that Vivian should be pleased with her and love her.

"I love you! I love you!" she would say as she waited in the wings.

It was Vivian who gave her the strength to do what was required.

It was not very arduous at first.

They were in a Play in which he was the star, and the audience applauded him.

Not because he was a particularly good actor, but because he was so handsome.

Then after seven years of acting in the West End and going on tour, which for Vivian's sake Rosie endured without complaining, the Gaiety Theatre came into being.

Vivian had been excited about it.

He talked incessantly about the new Theatre that was projected, but Rosie had taken very little interest.

She was finding it hard to keep the late hours which Vivian enjoyed.

She had to attend suppers after the Show, lasting long after midnight, and at the same time try to make a home for him.

In cheap, very uncomfortable lodgings this meant getting up early in the morning to have everything exactly as he liked it when he awoke.

Then she began to concentrate on what he was talking about.

A new Theatre, and therefore brighter, more airy, more comfortable and more sanitary than the existing Playhouse.

"They have been to Paris to inspect a number of the Paris Theatres," Vivian announced.

Rosie wondered who "they" were, but was not really interested enough to ask.

"They are going to call it 'The Gaiety Theatre'—a name which speaks for itself," Vivian said a little later. "It is to be in the Strand and under the direction of John Hollingshead."

"Would you like steak for supper tonight?" Rosie had asked.

She was intent on feeding Vivian well.

She made sure that he did not lose his looks as other actors did when they ate too little and drank too much.

"Yes, yes, of course," Vivian agreed.

But he was really thinking of the Theatre, and Rosie then began to realise that she must regard the Theatre as a more serious rival than anything she had encountered so far.

Of course she had often been jealous.

She would not have been human if she had not been jealous of the women who fawned on Vivian because he was so good-looking.

She was upset by the letters he received from the public.

But more worrying were the women in the Theatre.

They flirted with him with their eyes, their lips, and their bodies, whether Rosie was present or not.

He could not help making himself charming to everyone and anyone who praised him.

Meanwhile, the part he was playing at the moment at the Olympic had made him even more popular than before.

Rosie tried not to mind when he received an invitation to supper and she was not included.

She would go home alone to the flat they now had in Covent Garden.

She would lie awake, knowing that it was impossible to sleep until Vivian was beside her.

Sometimes he would creep in surreptitiously.

Because she knew he did not wish to be questioned and was hoping she would not be aware of how late he had come home, or rather how early in the morning, she would pretend to be asleep.

At other times he would come back full of excitement.

Almost before he was in the door he would start telling her what a success he had been.

He repeated the compliments he had been paid, and the interesting people he had met.

This was far more reassuring. She realised that no Lady of what she thought of secretly as "her own class" would ever have been seen with Vivian.

Although her husband might entertain them just as he entertained the pretty girls in the Theatre.

But all the time Vivian was making sure that Mr.

Hollingshead should decide that he could not put on a show at the Gaiety without him, and of course, Rosie.

By this time Rosie had grown used to playing the "bit parts" that required a very pretty but by no means dramatic actress.

In fact, she could not really act.

She was simply herself: sweet, gentle, and very lovely, but not in the least theatrical.

Some of the Producers grumbled and told her to "put some heart into it," but Vivian was quite content.

As long as his wife was earning enough money to enable them to live with some degree of luxury, he had no wish to find her rivalling Nellie Farren.

She was the female star who drew the audiences at the Olympic.

Nellie became the star at the Gaiety.

For the first time, the company included girls who were chosen not for their dramatic or vocal abilities but for their faces and their figures.

Most of them did not even have to speak.

They just had to look beautiful, and that Rosie could do without any difficulty.

"I suppose you know your wife is the most beautiful person on the stage today?" someone said to Vivian Vaughan.

"That is what I think," he replied with his charming smile.

"You are undoubtedly the most handsome juvenile lead, and that makes the two of you unique."

The way his admirer spoke gave Vivian an idea.

He went to Mr. Hollingshead and suggested that he and Rosie should be billed as "The Most Beautiful Couple on the London Stage"—or on any other stage for that matter.

Hollingshead was somewhat surprised, but finally

he realised this was a new idea and a clever one.

When he billed Vivian and Rosie as suggested, they were both a tremendous success.

By this time Rosie had blossomed and she was far more beautiful than she had been as a girl.

She had, however, lost some of her engaging shyness.

At the same time, her classical features and her good breeding marked her out as different from other girls.

Beautiful though they were, they were not as Vivian put it concisely, "out of the same stable."

Special songs were written for "The Most Beautiful Couple."

The applause they received every night became louder and more prolonged.

They might be a god and goddess from Olympus. Rosie looked ravishing in a very revealing Greek gown.

Or Vivian in an elaborate uniform would play the soldier saying good-bye to the woman he loved before a battle in which he was killed.

Then Rosie, lying prostrate on his grave, would weep because she had lost him, and every woman in the audience wiped the tears from her eyes.

They appeared in tableaux of many different types.

The only thing that really mattered was that Vivian was so handsome and Rosie looked so incredibly beautiful.

The smart young "Men about Town" had their opera-glasses trained on her from the moment she appeared.

Of course, she received a great many invitations from these gentlemen.

While she refused all those that did not include Vivian, she found it difficult to keep them from pursuing her and writing her letters which she threw on to the fire.

"Why can they never leave me alone?" she asked Vivian angrily.

"Because, my darling, you are every man's ideal of loveliness," he answered, "and you are certainly mine!"

She believed him because she wanted to.

But she was nevertheless beginning to have an uncomfortable feeling: The huge success he had become at the Gaiety had made his love for her less intense and less passionate than it had been in the past.

It was something she could not bear to admit, even to herself.

But she knew, if she were honest, that the nights when he explained that he was going to a stag-party and she must go home alone were becoming more and more frequent.

When she brushed his evening-clothes in the morning there would be powder on his shoulder and even a scent of perfume that was not the one she was using.

She told herself it was not important.

That everything was as wonderful as it had always been.

Yet the truth was that she was seeing less and less of Vivian.

Their only intimate contact with each other seemed to be when they appeared together on the stage.

At home he came in late and left early and was either querulous or else too tired to do anything but sleep.

Rosie could remember the very first time he said he had been invited away for the weekend.

"I knew you would understand, darling," he said.

He was using the charm which always made her

feel as if there were an audience watching them.

"Lord Thurston," he went on, "has asked me to join his house-party after the Show on Saturday night, and to stay until I have to be in the Theatre on Monday evening."

"After the . . . Show?" Rosie said stupidly. "But how will you get to the country so late?"

"Lord Thurston is taking his guests down in his private train," Vivian said airily, "and as it will not take more than an hour, we will have supper when we arrive."

It was the first time that Rosie had been alone on a Sunday.

Because she had nothing else to do she had gone to Church.

She had almost forgotten in the years of acting with Vivian how much Church services, held in the small Norman Church in which she had been christened, had meant to her as a girl.

She had prayed then for everything she wanted.

None of it seemed very important, and now she felt herself praying desperately that she would not lose Vivian.

She thought later that she must have had a premonition, for that was exactly what happened.

He told her a month later that he was going to America.

She could hardly believe what she was hearing and that he was not speaking in a foreign language.

"To . . . America?" she asked stupidly.

"There is someone there who has promised me, if I want it, a Theatre of my own, but first I intend to have a long holiday exploring the country I have heard so much about but never seen."

"You are . . . going . . . alone?"

Vivian looked away from her and she knew it was a stupid question.

Of course he was not going alone.

She knew that the rich American widow he had met staying at Lord Thurston's had been too big a temptation for him to refuse.

Once again her pride had prevented her from screaming and throwing herself at Vivian's feet and begging him not to leave her.

"I will leave some money for you in the Bank," he said, "and, as you know by this time, you are earning as much as I am."

That was one of the reasons that he was so eager to get away, Rosie thought.

She had been aware in the last few months that her popularity had somehow exceeded Vivian's.

She was not certain how or why it had happened.

But she had received more letters, more flowers, and more attention in subtle little ways, which it was now hard to remember, than he had.

She was quite certain, looking back, that it had rankled with him.

He wanted to be on his own, without having to bring her along as "The Most Beautiful Woman in the World."

It was all decided so quickly that only when he had gone did she realise that it had really happened and he had left her for ever.

One final blow had been even more difficult to assimilate.

She was packing his things, and the heavy stone in her breast prevented her from feeling anything but a kind of numbness that had deadened emotion in her.

She said to Vivian:

"Are you . . . going to . . . m-marry this woman?"

"I can hardly do that if I am married to you," he replied.

Then he paused in such a peculiar manner that, looking at him, Rosie had asked:

"What is . . . it? What is . . . troubling you?"

They had been too close to each other for her not to know that he was struggling with his conscience.

Or perhaps with a sense of decency which she had always thought was characteristic of him.

"I suppose I might as well come clean," he said. "I was married before I met you!"

"M-married?"

It did not sound to Rosie like her own voice saying the word:

"It was when I was very young," he said. "She was older than I was and when she went off with a rich man it did not surprise me."

"Are you . . . saying," Rosie faltered, "that . . . we are not . . . m-married?"

"What it comes down to is that I am a bigamist!" Vivian replied. "As I had not heard of or from my wife for five years, when I met you I presumed she was dead."

"And . . . was she?"

"Strangely enough, I heard of her last week when I read in the newspapers that the chap she had been with all those years had left her a fortune which was being contested by the children he had by another woman."

Rosie shut her eyes.

Somehow it did not seem true, but more than that, it did not seem real.

It was as if she were taking part in one of the many sketches they had acted together.

The whole thing was only "make-believe."

When Vivian had gone she realised her family had been right in thinking she had chosen a life of degradation.

She knew, even though she had been happy with him, that he had taken from her something very precious—her self-respect.

"How can it have happened to me?" Rosie asked.

It was a question women have asked since the beginning of time.

But it had.

She, Lady Rosamund Ormond, had been not the wife, but the mistress of an actor.

He had enticed her into a world of which she had known nothing, and which she admitted now did not compensate for all she had lost.

But it was too late, too late to change, too late to go back and admit she had made a mistake.

She was beautiful, she was a success with the public.

Rosie Rill was written in large letters on every handbill that advertised the Gaiety.

"I will show them that I am as good as they are, if not better!" Rosie told herself defiantly.

That was exactly what in her own way she had done, and yet where had it brought her?

To her fifty-sixth birthday, with only two cards to celebrate it.

A small bunch of cheap flowers that had been presented to her by Amy, her dresser, who had retired when she had.

"I hate everything! I hate this boring life and I wish I were dead!" Rosie said beneath her breath.

Then as she spoke inaudibly the words which came from her heart, the door opened and Amy came in.

"There's someone to see you, Miss Rosie!"

"Who is it?" Rosie asked.

"She wouldn't give 'er name, but she says she's your niece and she wants to see you ever so important-like."

"My niece?"

Rosie stared at Amy in astonishment.

She tried to think who it was who had played her

niece in the last performance she had given at the Gaiety.

They had written in a sketch for her simply because the public loved "Our Rosie," as they called her, but she had never been an actress.

She could not get across a heavier, more tempestuous part that required an older woman.

Somebody must have played her niece in the sketch—but who was it?

Surely, she thought, she could not be so old that she could not remember a simple thing like that!

"Well? Will you see 'er, or won't you?" Amy asked.

"Oh, show her in," Rosie replied. "Anything is better than sitting here thinking of the past!"

She might as well talk to some stage-struck young girl as to nobody.

There was a pause before Amy reappeared.

"'Ere she is!" she said brightly. "An' she says her name's Ina Wescott."

Slowly Rosie turned her head.

A very young and, she thought, nervous girl was coming in through the door.

"Thank you," said the girl in a soft voice to Amy as she passed her.

She then proceeded across the room.

Rosie stared at her in astonishment, wondering if she had gone mad or was having an hallucination.

For walking towards her was herself just as she had been nearly forty years ago.

chapter two

FOR a moment Rosie could only stare.

Then in a voice that did not sound like her own she asked:

"Who . . . are you?"

"I am your . . . niece," the girl answered in a frightened little voice, "and it may seem . . . impertinent . . . but . . . I have come to you for . . . help."

"For help?" Rosie echoed, feeling as if her brain had stopped functioning and she could not think clearly.

Then unexpectedly the girl smiled and it seemed to make her face radiant as she said:

"I am so . . . thrilled to meet you, I have heard about . . . you so often, and to me you have always been the most . . . exciting person in the . . . world!"

"H-how could I be?" Rosie asked.

Then as if she suddenly realised the girl who

looked so like herself was still standing while she was sitting, she said:

"Sit down, my dear, and tell me what all this is about. It has taken me by surprise and I feel a little bewildered."

"I was very . . . frightened in case you would not see . . . me."

"Suppose we start at the beginning," Rosie suggested, "and tell me exactly who you are."

"I am the daughter of your youngest sister, Averil."

"Averil!"

Rosie remembered as she spoke that Averil had been a very little girl when she had run away from home.

She had been a pretty, blue-eyed child still in the Nursery, while her second sister, Muriel, had just been promoted to the School-Room.

"So you are Averil's daughter!" she said after a moment. "Tell me about her."

Ina looked at Rosie for a moment, then she said:

"You do not know that Mama is . . . dead?"

"I am sorry, I had no idea of it."

"And now . . . Papa is . . . dead too," Ina went on, "and I have nowhere to go. I thought . . . if you were not too busy . . . you might . . . help me find . . . something to do so that I can keep . . . myself."

Rosie looked at Ina as if she could not believe what she had heard. Then she said:

"Are you telling me that your mother has left you no money? What about your grandfather—I know he is alive."

Rosie knew this because in the long days when she had nothing to do and nobody to talk to she read the Court columns of the newspapers and the Social articles in the Women's Magazines.

Occasionally they mentioned her father because he was Lord Lieutenant of Hertfordshire, as he had been for many years.

"I believe my grandfather is alive," Ina replied, "but I suppose you do not know that Mama was cut off from the family because, like you, she ran away with somebody she loved."

"Your mother ran away?" Rosie repeated, feeling it could not be true.

Ina smiled, and it made her look so like the reflection Rosie had seen in her mirror when she was that age that it was uncanny.

"Mama did not run away with anybody so exciting and dashing as you did," Ina said, "but with a Curate of the Church in the Park. Do you remember the Church?"

"Yes, of course I remember it," Rosie replied.

"Papa was not as handsome as Mr. Vaughan, but he was very good-looking. I used to tease him and say that the women in our Parish came to Church only so that they could stare at him and hope he would pay them some attention."

"So Averil married a Parson!"

"Mama told me how furious Grandpapa was when she told him she was in love. He raged at her and said that if she married Papa, she could leave his house and never come back!"

Ina looked at Rosie apprehensively before she went on.

"He added that he had had one daughter who had made a disastrous marriage and he was not going to have another one."

"That sounds very like my father!" Rosie said in a hard voice.

"He was very cruel to Mama, and forbade her to see Papa again. He then complained to the Bishop, who transferred Papa to a small village in the wilds of Gloucestershire."

"But your Mama followed him?"

"They eloped most romantically," Ina replied, "and were married as they travelled towards the village to which he had just been appointed Vicar. They expected Grandpapa would follow them and try to take Mama back."

"But he did not do so," Rosie said.

She felt that she knew exactly what happened.

"Mama told me they heard nothing until they had a letter from Grandpapa saying she had forfeited the right to be his daughter, and not only would her name never be mentioned again in his hearing, but she would never receive one penny of his money!"

Rosie shut her eyes.

She could remember only too well what she had felt when she received a similar letter.

How apologetic she had been to Vivian, because he had obviously expected she would have at least enough money of her own to buy her clothes.

"That, of course," Ina went on, "meant that Papa and Mama were very poor, but they were so happy that it did not seem to matter."

"Really happy?" Rosie asked.

"I do not think any two people could have been happier," Ina replied. "It was only when I got older that Mama used to say she was sorry she could not give me things that she had had as a girl like horses, carriages, beautiful clothes, parties, and Balls. . . ."

"And, of course, a great number of friends of our own social standing," Rosie said almost beneath her breath.

Ina laughed and it was a very young and happy sound.

"I do not think Mama minded at all not having

25

those things because she was so happy with Papa. Our little Vicarage was pretty and comfortable, and I never remember worrying about money...until now...."

She gave Rosie a frightened look from her deep blue eyes and in a low voice she said:

"That is why I have...come to see...you."

"And you really think I can help you?"

"There is no one else," Ina said. "Papa had no money apart from his stipend, so now that he is dead I...must earn enough to eat...if nothing...else."

She tried to speak lightly.

There was, however, a note in her voice that told Rosie she was really afraid of the future.

"I suppose, my dear, if you went to see your grandfather he might forgive you for the 'sins of your parents' and welcome you into the fold."

"I do not think that is likely," Ina answered. "Papa wrote and told him when Mama died simply because he thought it was the courteous way to behave."

"And what happened?"

"Papa's letter was sent back with the contents torn in half."

Rosie drew in her breath.

"That was a despicable thing to do!"

"Papa was very hurt...and I know if Mama had been alive, she would have...cried."

Ina spoke quite simply, and there was a pause before Rosie said:

"So you have come to me because there is nobody else."

"Absolutely nobody!" Ina agreed. "In any case, I have always wanted to know you because I thought it was so brave and wonderful of you to elope as Mama did and become so famous with your husband."

Rosie's lips tightened before she said:

"How can you possibly know that? I cannot believe your father and mother talked about me."

Ina looked at her for a long moment, and there was just a touch of colour in her pale cheeks before she said:

"I think . . . although it seems strange . . . that Papa was . . . shocked because you were on . . . the stage. But Mama used to talk about you when we were alone."

She paused and gave a sigh.

"She told me how beautiful you were and how everybody admired you and how Grandpapa had expected you would make a very important marriage to somebody as distinguished as himself."

Rosie did not speak and Ina clasped her hands together as she said:

"To me it was the most romantic story I could imagine, and after Mama told me about you I used to look for you in the newspapers and read about you in the magazines."

"Your mother talked to you about me?" Rosie said almost beneath her breath.

"I think the reason she was brave enough to run away with Papa was that she knew how happy and successful you have been."

Rosie gasped.

Then as if she were afraid of pursuing that subject she said:

"You must tell me exactly what you think I could do for you."

Ina looked shy, then she said:

"It may seem very presumptuous of me . . . but I thought as you are so famous . . . you might find me something . . . to do in the Theatre . . . if not on the stage . . . at the back, sewing . . . or helping."

Then as she felt Rosie did not understand, she said:

"I am sure I am too young to be a Governess and I

have no talent for which ... anyone would ... pay me."

Again there was a pause.

Rosie was thinking it would not be difficult to set up so beautiful a girl at the Gaiety.

But she remembered the agonies she had suffered when at Ina's age she had first on Vivian's insistence appeared behind the footlights.

In recent years after leaving the Gaiety she had been alone day after day with nothing to interest her.

Her friends, and there had been precious few of them, came to see her less and less.

It was then she bitterly regretted that mad moment when she had left the safety and security of her home, her family, and her position as the daughter of an Earl for a handsome actor.

How, she wondered, could she tell this child, looking so exactly like herself, of the endless struggle it was to keep in the public eye.

To be sure of getting a role which was a step up rather than a step down, in the next Play, the next Show, and the one after that.

How could she tell this young, innocent girl from a Vicarage what endless temptations there were.

Which, while she thought she was Vivian's wife, she had resisted, simply because she loved him.

Even then it had not been easy.

At times she had been afraid not only of the passion men felt for her, but also lest refusing them might affect her position with the Management of the Theatre.

They wanted more than anything else for their important patrons to be satisfied.

Then when Vivian left her and she learned that she was not even his wife, she had thought first that her life was over and the sooner she died the better.

He had gone away at the end of the Show and there was a week of rehearsals before the next one opened.

Having cried for two days, Rosie had even gone down to the River Thames and looked at the dark swirling water.

She thought if it closed over her head she would no longer have to go on suffering for a man who did not want her.

Then that strange pride, which had shown itself first in the Ormonds at the Battle of Agincourt, showed itself again.

The pride which had made them struggle for positions of power at Court.

The pride which made them receive one Royal award after another made her know that she would not allow Vivian or anybody else to defeat her.

She had gone to the Gaiety, persuaded Mr. Hollingshead to write in a part for her without Vivian.

She then set out with a new, hard determination.

It was to show the man who had left her that she could do without him.

Every time she was applauded, every commendation she earned from the critics, every compliment she received she felt was somehow a gesture of defiance to the man she had loved so desperately.

He had left her for a woman who had more money than she had.

"That is what counts ultimately," she told herself bitterly, "just money!"

Not love, not devotion, not self-sacrifice, but golden sovereigns.

Slowly but progressively, instead of the soft, sweet, gentle Rosie Rill who had portrayed with Vivian "The Most Beautiful Couple in the World," there had emerged somebody very different.

Beautiful, but no longer sitting adoringly at a man's feet.

A woman determined, however difficult it might be, to stand on her own.

But Fate had one more blow to deal Rosie, and it came to her, of course, in the shape of a man.

At first she had to force herself, however unwillingly, to accept invitations to the supper-parties she had always refused before unless Vivian was included.

Yet because she was so lovely and now obviously unencumbered, the invitations multiplied.

The profusion of flowers in her dressing-room made it a fragrant bower.

At first, because she was so desperately unhappy, she was careful to accept invitations only where there would be several men and other girls from the Gaiety, which made it a party.

Then, as might have been expected, she met the Marquis of Colthaust.

She had read about him, of course, and she had seen him in the same box at the Theatre night after night.

Although she paid little attention to them, she had heard stories of how he entertained the most beautiful of the Gaiety Girls.

They had no complaints about his generosity.

What she had not observed, concentrating too completely on Vivian to think of any other man, was that the Marquis's conquests, if that was what they were, never lasted for very long.

He finally asked her out to supper, saying that there was a party, and that when the Show was over he would collect her at the stage-door.

When she found him he drove her not to Romano's, as she had expected, but to his house in Grosvenor Square.

It never struck her that this was a privilege which was not accorded to other women from the Gaiety.

That there was in fact anything unusual in his taking her to supper at his own house.

What she did find strange was that when they arrived, there was nobody else there except themselves.

She had looked at him enquiringly, and the Marquis explained:

"I want to talk to you, Rosie, or should I say 'Rosamund'?"

She had stiffened and he said:

"It took me some time to discover the truth of who you were, but now I can see a likeness to other members of your family."

Rosie had turned away from him petulantly.

"I do not want to talk about my family," she said, "and I am quite certain they would not talk to you about me."

"I think it was extremely brave of you to run away with Vaughan," the Marquis said, "and I consider it very wrong of him to have left you."

"I do not want your pity, or anybody else's!" Rosie snapped.

"I can understand your feeling like that," the Marquis agreed, "but because you are different from other women at the Gaiety, I want you to talk to me about yourself."

He stopped talking to look at her.

"I want, too, to understand how you could love a man like Vaughan, who was completely alien to the life you knew before you met him."

She had told herself she would never talk to anyone about what had happened.

Yet there was something about the Marquis that she found irresistible.

For the first time since Vivian had left her she told

31

him how much she had suffered.

She told him, because he seemed to understand, how many difficulties there had been in the years they were together.

Adjusting herself to Vivian's way of life, Vivian's interests, and to Vivian himself.

Although she did not realise it at first, she was aware of the difference between a handsome but quite ordinary young man, who came from a different class than herself, and an aristocrat like the Marquis.

She knew it was something she could not put into words.

But she was tinglingly aware of him.

Yet, because her life had consisted of one man and one man only for so long, she did not realise that he was wooing her in a very subtle way.

So she fell in love.

Of course she fell in love! How could she resist a man to whom she could talk as an equal, who made her feel like a goddess in front of the footlights, and not just behind them?

The Marquis was not so foolish as to "rush his fences."

They had a quiet supper together.

When it was over he took her home, kissed her hand, and left her at the door of her lodgings.

It was not until they had seen each other every day for nearly two weeks that Rosie admitted to herself that she was in love with him.

She loved with all the conviction and passion of a woman rather than the infatuation of a romantic School-girl.

The Marquis bought a house for her in St. John's Wood, and she furnished it with the good taste that was instinctive in her.

It had lain dormant during the years of moving from lodgings to lodgings and finally to a flat in Covent Garden that was already furnished.

This was her own, and she loved it just as she loved the Marquis.

She half-expected he would ask her to give up her role at the Gaiety.

That was until she understood that it was very much a part of his life.

He enjoyed having his box waiting for him night after night.

After spending what he told her were dull hours in the House of Lords dining with Statesmen or at Marlborough House with the Prince of Wales, he wanted to be amused.

He would often not arrive until the last act at the Gaiety.

When she had changed to one of her evening-gowns and wrapped the sables he had given her round her shoulders, she would find his carriage waiting for her at the stage-door.

He seemed to make everything they did together exciting and in some way magical.

She finally admitted to herself that she loved him even more than she had ever loved Vivian.

She then began to pray with a desperation that came from her soul that he would marry her.

She could imagine nothing more wonderful than to be the Marquis's wife.

She would leave forever the garishness of the Gaiety, and be utterly content to be the chatelaine of his huge ancestral home in the country.

She could entertain in the exquisitely furnished rooms in Grosvenor Square.

She imagined herself sitting at the end of his table wearing the Colthaust diamonds.

They were far more outstanding than anything her mother had ever possessed.

She would see amazement in her father's eyes when he realised that despite his ostracism his daughter's husband was more socially important than he was himself.

"Please God, let Lionel ask me . . . please, God . . . please. . . ."

When he went to the country at weekends, she went to Church and prayed that anything wrong she had done in her life would be forgiven and that God would be merciful to her now.

For over a year she was blissfully happy and so deeply in love that her happiness seemed to radiate from her when she was on the stage.

She became more popular with the audiences than she had ever been before.

She had a full-length picture in every magazine, and the critics mentioned her every time they wrote about the Gaiety.

Mr. Hollingshead gave her better parts and even better clothes to wear.

"You are the epitome, Rosie, of everything the Gaiety stands for," he said once, "for everything I am trying to educate the public into appreciating."

He smiled at her.

She was thinking as he did so that she must remember exactly what he had said so that she could repeat it to the Marquis.

Then the blow fell.

After Christmas the Marquis told her that in February he intended going to Monte Carlo.

She knew he had a Villa there.

She had heard him talk so often of the amusements, the gaiety, of Monte Carlo and how fashionable it was so that even the Prince and Princess of Wales were regular visitors.

She waited for him to invite her to go with him.

As the days passed and he said nothing, she realised with almost a sense of shock that he intended to go alone.

"You will not be away for long, will you?" she asked.

"It all depends upon how amusing I find it," he replied. "Last year I stayed for only a week."

Her spirits rose and she told herself that she must not intrude on a part of his life that was separate from what he spent with her.

He seemed to be very busy just before he left.

Yet he was with her most nights and she was happier than she had ever been before.

"You are very beautiful, Rosie," he said.

They were lying in the large comfortable bed that seemed almost to fill the small bedroom of her house.

"The only thing that is important is that you should think so," Rosie answered, and knew it was the truth.

The applause she had received that night was gratifying only because the Marquis was there in his box, watching and listening.

Six times she had been called in front of the curtain and there had been huge baskets of orchids lifted up onto the stage.

Finally she waved good-bye to the cheering audience, and carried with her only a bouquet of red roses which the Marquis had sent her.

When she reached her dressing-room she found hidden among the stems a bracelet of turquoises and diamonds.

She felt a little thrill run through her as she put it on her wrist and changed hastily.

She had run down the iron staircase to the stage-door and the Marquis was waiting for her.

He looked magnificent in his evening-cape with its red lining thrown back over his shoulders.

There was one perfect pearl pinned to the front of his starched white shirt.

She felt her love for him well up in her heart like a tidal wave.

"How can you be so kind, so wonderful to me?" she asked as she stepped into his carriage.

"I thought the bracelet would become you," he said in his deep voice.

They dined at Romano's.

Because she was so in love, Rosie had felt as if everybody else was envying her being partnered by the most distinguished man in London.

When they had gone back to St. John's Wood, she imagined, though it had been only a fleeting thought, that he had looked at her in a somewhat strange and unusual way.

Their love-making had been passionate.

Because she was so happy, Rosie felt as if he carried her up to the stars.

"I love you! I love you!" she said.

It just flashed through her mind that if only now he would ask her to be his wife it would be the most wonderful and perfect thing she had ever known.

He left her a little earlier than usual.

She thought it was because he had a long journey ahead of him the following day and had no wish to be tired.

He had kissed her very gently, but without passion, as he said:

"Take care of yourself, Rosie, my dear."

Then he had gone down the stairs to let himself out to where his carriage was waiting for him.

'He will not be away for long,' Rosie thought confidently before she fell asleep.

The next day there had been a letter to tell her that everything between them was finished.

She could hardly believe what she read.

Yet she had known with some instinct that could not be denied that it was the sort of letter he had written a dozen times before.

He thanked her for the happiness they had enjoyed together.

He knew she would understand that even the best things in life cannot continue forever.

But how could Rosie begin to understand that she had lost him when she loved him so completely and absolutely?

She did not cry, she only felt suddenly as if everything in her body had been turned to stone.

She had no feelings, and her brain had somehow ceased to function.

She had gone to the Theatre, moving like an automaton, walking through her part as if she were no longer a real person.

She was a puppet with some invisible hand pulling the strings by which she moved.

She was not even aware that the other performers seemed to avoid her.

When they encountered her in the passages they were in a hurry to get away.

It was Amy who told her, Amy her dresser, who had been with her for three years.

Amy gave her an affection which at the same time had a stringent quality about it that invariably made her tell the truth.

No one else in the Theatre had mentioned the Marquis to Rosie, but Amy said as she was getting ready to go home alone:

"Now, don't you go breakin' yer 'eart over that man as ain't no good to you, nor to any other woman as is stupid enough to lose 'er 'eart to 'im, as that young Millie'll soon find out!"

The last few words made Rosie stare at Amy in a bemused manner.

"What do you mean by that?" she asked.

"She's the new girl as comes on as 'Spring' in the first 'alf, and is in the tableau as 'Diana the Huntress.'"

"What has she got to do with the Marquis?" Rosie asked in a voice that did not sound like her own.

"You'd better ask 'er when she gets back from Monte Carlo!" Amy answered. "'Is Nibs 'as persuaded the Boss into lettin' 'er take a week off. Some people 'as all the luck!"

"I do not believe it!" Rosie cried.

She knew the girl in question was a newcomer to the Show.

Because Millie had seemed so young and so inexperienced, she had gone out of her way to speak kindly to her.

She might be as frightened as she herself had been the first time she appeared at the Olympic with Vivian.

After Rosie understood that her romance, for that was what it had been to her, was finished, the business side of it became apparent.

She was given a month by the Marquis's Solicitors to quit the house in St. John's Wood.

He had told her it was for her.

She had been far too foolish to ask if the Lease was in her name and if it really belonged to her.

She suspected that, as it was so beautifully furnished, the Marquis would soon install another occupant in it.

It was then that Rosie had sworn two things.

First, that she would never give her heart to any man again.

Second, that she would have enough money to buy everything she wanted, money which Vivian had already told her was more important than love.

The Marquis had been generous, and she had received quite a large amount of cash from him.

But she had been stupid enough to pay for some gowns herself, things for the house, food, and drink when it seemed too petty to present him with small accounts.

"That is something I will never do again!" Rosie vowed.

After that she never allowed her heart to rule her head, and she sold herself dearly.

In the years that followed there had been men who succeeded each other in what seemed, looking back, to be a procession of millionaires.

They begged for her favours and she could pick and choose.

What influenced them most was that a man gained the admiration of his friends and much kudos if he acquired Rosie as his mistress.

She made certain of the old adage that a man appreciates what he has to pay for, and where Rosie was concerned, they paid, and went on paying.

Never again did she buy anything for herself.

The house in which she lived, her clothes, her food, her servants, her jewelry, her dresser—all were paid for and generously.

Just as Mr. Hollingshead dressed her for the stage, her lovers dressed her for the world outside.

There was no one at the Gaiety who had finer jewels, better furs, or more outstanding clothes.

Expensive rings bedecked the fingers of her hands; a sable rug covered her knees in her carriage drawn by two superb horses.

The livery of her servants rivalled that of Royalty.

She was the talk of London and, if she had wished

to leave the Gaiety, a dozen other Theatres were open to her.

Then, when she reached her fortieth birthday, she knew that the "writing was on the wall."

She had never been an actress, her success lay entirely in her looks.

Even grease-paint could not disguise the lines or the fact that she was no longer the Spring-time fairy-tale goddess she had appeared to be for so long.

Proudly, when she was forty-five, and because she took such care of herself that she looked nearly ten years younger, Rosie left the Gaiety.

She knew better than any impresario that she could not act the parts that might have been offered to her.

She was not an actress, she was a "Gaiety Girl," which was a very different thing.

She had taken part in small sketches if they were cleverly written and she did not have to do anything emotional or dramatic.

She simply had to look beautiful and outrageously smart in gowns that disguised the fact that her arms and hands were getting older and that her chin-line was beginning to sag.

Again that pride which had carried her through so much in her life told her that it was time to "bring down the curtain."

This time on herself rather than let it fall down.

She left at the end of the current Show.

She was not surprised when George Edwardes, who had taken Mr. Hollingshead's place, did not press her to join the cast of the next production which was to open in three weeks' time.

She had already decided to refuse any invitations.

When in fact none materialised, it made her feel only more bitter than she was already.

All the bitterness of the years sat with her when she was alone in the charming flat overlooking Regent's Park.

Her last lover had paid for it and she had made quite certain he could not take it away from her when their liaison broke up.

"Mine, mine!" she had told herself.

She knew it was a very small and poor compensation for everything she had lost.

At first, because they were curious, people with whom she had performed came to see her.

"When are you coming back to the stage, Rosie?" they would ask.

"I am enjoying myself doing nothing," she replied, and they had believed her.

Gradually, however, her visitors grew fewer and fewer and the invitations to luncheon or dinner ceased altogether.

"I am alone, completely alone!"

The bitterness had become so much a part of her thinking and breathing that she would not have known herself without it.

Now with a start Rosie realised that Ina was looking at her.

She was waiting for an answer to her question as to what she could do.

She could see the fear in her blue eyes that were so much like her own.

She could also sense the fluttering in Ina's breast because she was alone.

If her aunt failed her, she had no idea what she would do next.

Then as she looked at the girl, so lovely, so untouched, so like herself, Rosie knew almost as if somebody had told her that here was an instrument for revenge.

An instrument to repay all she had suffered had been placed in her hands.

She would be a fool not to use it.

She would revenge herself on those who had hurt her, those who had left her alone with nothing to console her except her memories.

"I will show them!"

They were words that had rung so often in her ears, and they were ringing once again.

Aloud she said with a smile, which for the moment swept away the hardness of the lines around her lips and the tiredness in her eyes:

"But, of course, Ina dear, you must stay here with me, and I shall be very happy to have you!"

chapter three

ROSIE had been intelligent enough when she was beginning to accumulate money to go to a good Stock-
broker.

One of her lovers, an extremely rich Banker, had
said that the Broker he employed was the cleverest
man in London.

She had therefore consulted him and after that left
everything in his capable hands.

He had trebled her money in ten years.

By the time she left the stage she was an extremely rich woman because she had saved everything she was given.

When she was finally alone she was careful with
every penny, simply because cheese-paring had become part of her life.

Anyway, there was little besides her clothes and
food on which she needed to spend money.

Amy looked after her in the flat.

Rosie had a cook who came in every day to prepare her meals which were not elaborate.

The woman also cleaned everything Amy left for her.

Now Rosie realised she had a purpose in spending, and it was a very good one.

All the years she had been in the Theatre she had deliberately kept the name of her family secret, and had forced Vivian to do the same.

Later she had made the Marquis give her his word of honour that what he had discovered about her would never be told to anybody else.

He had understood that it was her pride that refused to allow her to drag her family down from the pinnacle on which they had set themselves.

He told her how much he respected her, knowing few women would have behaved in the same way.

But the Marquis had left her, and only six months later he was married.

When Rosie opened the newspaper and saw the announcement of his engagement to the daughter of a Duke, she thought she must faint.

She had longed more than she had longed for anything in her whole life that he would ask her to be his wife.

Instead, once again something else had proved more important than love.

In this instance not money, but blood.

It took Rosie quite a long time to plan exactly how she would use Ina for her revenge.

She was aware every minute of the day they were together that the girl was more and more like herself as she had been when she was eighteen.

Because Ina had lived in the country, everything that she saw in London and everything they did was an excitement and delight.

She was thrilled with the traffic in the streets, the smart horses and carriages with their distinguished owners, and the riders in Rotten Row.

She was enchanted with the shops and almost speechless with delight when Rosie took her to the dressmakers.

First Rosie had stood in front of her mirror and considered her reflection.

She was not looking at Rosie Rill, the star of the Gaiety, but at Lady Rosamund Ormond, daughter of the Earl of Ormond and Staverley.

Her father, who had condemned her all those years ago, was now an old man of nearly eighty, but he would still be shocked and disturbed at what she intended to do.

She wanted to hurt him as he had hurt her.

Looking at herself in the mirror, she realised that beneath the mascara, the rouge, and the powder, there was still the beauty of her straight, classical nose and her oval forehead.

When she smiled, the lines at the corners of her mouth disappeared.

The charm that had captivated thousands of Theatre-goers was still there.

She washed her face and looked at herself again and for a moment she felt naked.

Then she knew that Lady Rosamund Ormond could look distinguished and, if she wished, very much a Lady.

Her hair had been dyed so that it was as fair as it had always been.

She ordered her hairdresser, who could hardly believe his ears, that she wanted him to tint it grey, until the grey hairs grew in naturally.

"What are you up to, Miss Rill?" he asked impertinently. "You won't look like yourself if you try to look old."

"I am not just trying," Rosie replied quietly, "I am old, and I wish to look my age."

When he had finished she realised she did look her age.

But in some ways more attractive than when she was trying desperately to cling to a youth that had passed.

She was still slim because she had never been a large eater.

The gowns she chose from the most expensive dressmaker in Hanover Square accentuated her figure without trying to make it vulgarly provocative.

"It's a pleasure to dress you, Miss Rill," the Manageress had said in all sincerity.

Rosie knew that she looked very much like the other customers who patronised the shop.

Most of them were ladies whose social life revolved round the Prince and Princess of Wales at Marlborough House.

Their photographs were to be seen in every high-class magazine.

Ina was easy.

Rosie bought for the girl the most beautiful and elaborate débutante gowns.

They were a good deal more expensive than those that most of the girls who were coming to London for the Season could afford.

"How can you give me anything so beautiful?" Ina asked. "I feel as if I am the Princess in a Fairy Story."

"That is exactly how I want you to feel," Rosie answered. "You must always remember that from now on you are a Princess and behave like one."

Ina smiled at her.

It was the same smile with which Rosie had captivated so many audiences.

"You are certainly my Fairy Godmother," she said softly, "and I am very, very grateful."

Rosie felt that this particular conversation was one that echoed down the years.

But she steeled her heart to remember that the only thing that mattered was that Ina should be taught to play her part in a Play.

It would not be enacted behind the footlights, but in real life.

Although the child was not aware of it, it would be highly dramatic and emotional.

When her clothes were ready, Rosie paid the bills without even counting up the total.

She then announced that they were leaving in three days for Monte Carlo.

Ina had given a cry of sheer delight.

"Monte Carlo! How wonderful! That is one place I have always longed to see! But Papa often said that many people, including the Bishops, thought it wicked because there was so much gambling there."

"The gambling will not affect you," Rosie said, "but everybody of importance will be in the Casino after dinner, and we will join them."

She was aware that Amy was biting back a dozen questions because Ina was in the room.

Rosie had already told her to curb her tongue when the girl was present.

As soon as they were alone Amy asked:

"Wot are you up to now, I'd like to know?"

"I am launching Miss Ina on the Social World!"

Amy looked at her shrewdly and after a few moments she said:

"You don't deceive me!"

"Well, you will have to wait to see what happens," Rosie replied.

Amy, however, was not content with this.

"You're up to somethin' naughty, Miss Rosie, and I wants to know wot it is!"

"If you want to accompany us to Monte Carlo," Rosie said sharply, "will you please wear the black clothes I bought for you and behave as a lady's-maid."

"If I don't know my duties at my time of life," Amy retorted, "then I never will!"

"It is not your duties I worry about," Rosie replied, "but the things you say. As I have told you before, well-behaved lady's-maids keep their thoughts to themselves, which is something you have never been able to do."

"I'm too old to change!" Amy snapped.

Rosie laughed.

"Then keep your thoughts silent until you and I are alone together. Then you can say what you like."

"Thanks for your permission!" Amy retorted sourly.

She went out of the room, slamming the door.

But Rosie knew that she would have allowed nothing to prevent her from accompanying them to Monte Carlo.

Then, at Victoria, they stepped into the train which was to carry them to Dover.

Amy wore her black bonnet set squarely on her grey hair, and carried Lady Rosamund's jewel-case complete with coronet.

She looked so exactly the part that she might have stepped straight off the stage of the Gaiety.

"From now on, I am going to use my own name," Rosie had announced the night before they left, "and you will please forget that I am Rosie Rill who once, a long time ago, was a star of the Gaiety Theatre."

"I could never forget that, Aunt Rosamund," Ina said impulsively, "and I am sure those who have seen you will never forget how beautiful you were. I have read in the newspapers how many curtain-calls you always had because the audience loved you."

"That is all in the past," Rosie said firmly. "Now I am myself, and it is something I want you both to remember."

She did not tell them, however, that she had sent an anonymous note to the two leading newspapers in Monte Carlo.

It informed them that Lady Rosamund Ormond, formerly Miss Rosie Rill of the Gaiety Theatre, was arriving at the Hôtel de Paris with her niece, Miss Ina Wescott, who was the granddaughter of the Ninth Earl of Ormond and Staverley.

She was quite certain that Journalists would be waiting when they stepped out of the sleeper-train.

She was not mistaken.

A photographer asked her to pose, but she swept past him disdainfully.

When they were in the carriage that was to take them to the Hôtel de Paris, she ignored the Pressmen who clustered around the door, saying:

"Why have you come to Monte Carlo, Miss Rill? Is it true that your real name is Lady Rosamund Ormond?"

"I tells you they'll never forget you!" Amy said with satisfaction as they drove away.

"They were very excited to see you, Aunt Rosamund," Ina exclaimed.

They were bowed into one of the best suites at the Hôtel de Paris, with balconies looking out over the harbour and beyond it to the sea.

"It is so beautiful and exactly how I thought it would be," Ina exclaimed.

She gazed in wonder at the magnificent yachts on the vividly blue sea below, the flowers that bloomed on the terraces.

They could glimpse the Palace standing on the high point beyond the harbour.

"Lovely! Lovely! Lovely!" Ina exclaimed. "How

49

can I ever thank you, Aunt Rosamund, for bringing me here?"

Rosie did not answer.

She was looking through the *Journal de Monaco* seeing with satisfaction the paragraph she had sent herself.

LADY ROSAMUND ORMOND, DAUGHTER OF THE 9TH EARL OF ORMOND AND STAVERLEY, WILL BE ARRIVING AT THE HÔTEL DE PARIS WITH HER NIECE, MISS INA WESCOTT.

LADY ROSAMUND ORMOND WAS BETTER KNOWN AS ROSIE RILL, THE STAR OF THE GAIETY THEATRE, AND MANY WILL REMEMBER HER SUCCESSES IN THE FOLLOWING SHOWS:

"ALI BABA," "THE BOHEMIAN GIRL," "ISLAND OF BACHELORS," "THE HYPOCRITE."

Rosie knew the paragraph would be read and re-read by everybody in Monte Carlo.

Interest would grow during the day as quite a number of people would be looking for their first appearance.

"How soon can we go out and explore, Aunt Rosamund?" Ina asked as Amy began to unpack.

"We are going to stay here," Rosie replied, "until this evening."

"Until this evening?" Ina questioned incredulously.

"Yes, dear, then we will dine downstairs and afterwards visit the Casino."

"But, Aunt Rosamund, the sun is shining and there is so much to see!"

"You will have plenty of time later to see it, and as I am tired and Amy is far too busy to accompany you, you will stay here."

"Of course . . . if that is what you wish," Ina said quietly, even though she was disappointed. "I will go and help Amy unpack."

There was certainly a great deal of it to do.

The number of trunks they had brought with them seemed enormous.

Ina's new gowns filled the wardrobe in her bed-room as well as a cupboard in the passage which connected her room to the Sitting-Room.

She could hardly believe it was true.

She kept running to the window to have another look at the yachts moving in and out of the harbour.

At the sea that seemed to become bluer as the day wore on, and the flag flying in the breeze on top of the Palace.

It was all so enchanting.

She chafed a little at being kept in when there was so much to see outside.

But she knew it would be ungrateful to question anything that her aunt decided, considering how kind she had been.

How could she have guessed, or even hoped, that when she called on her aunt she would welcome her.

Also dress her and bring her to Monte Carlo, of all places in the world?

* * *

Lying on her bed in another room, Rosie was care-fully reading the list of guests who were staying in the Principality.

A great many of them were English, including the Duke and Duchess of Marlborough, Lord Victor Paget, Lord Farquhar.

There were, too, the black-bearded Duke of Nor-folk, the Earl of Rosslyn, and Lily Langtry.

She read among the arrivals there was the King of

Wurkemberg, the Grand Dukes Serge and Boris of Russia, the Grand Duke of Luxembourg, and Prince Kotchoubey.

Rosie remembered he always had a pet dachshund with him, while Prince Mirza Riza Kahn of Persia wore a fez.

She read the names aloud, then stopped and stared as if to make sure she was not imagining what she saw.

THE MARQUIS OF COLTHAUST ACCOMPANIED BY HIS SON VISCOUNT COLT.

This was what she had hoped for, and her luck was in.

He was here, here in Monte Carlo, and what she had wanted more than anything else was that the Viscount Colt should be with him.

It was Amy who brought her the news from the Gaiety when she was too proud to try to obtain it herself.

Several times in the long years since she had shut herself off from the theatrical world because she could no longer glitter as a star she would watch a performance without anybody being aware of who she was.

She had disguised herself very cleverly with dark glasses.

There was a veil to cover her face, and wearing quiet, unobtrusive clothes which no one would notice, she would sit in the back row of the stalls.

From there she had seen the Gaiety Girls parading in exactly the same way as she had for so many years.

Watching the sketches in which she had been such a success because everybody was looking at her face rather than at her performance, she had not felt she was missing anything.

She had not even felt sentimental over the "good old days."

Nor was she envious of the flowers that were received by the new star.

She was not jealous of the applause which greeted the new girls, who were reported to be even more beautiful than they had ever been.

All she felt was a bitterness.

She had now lost both worlds in which she had once had a definite place, a definite part to play.

Because she remembered so vividly her home— the great mansion surrounded by her father's five-thousand acres of land, that the Gaiety, even though she had spent so many years of her life in it, seemed more unreal.

She was, as she had always been, a little alien to it.

There had been only two men in her life who had mattered.

First Vivian Vaughan, who was now dead. She had read of his death from a heart-attack three years ago!

It had meant nothing to her.

Nothing more than the memory of a handsome face that had lured her away from everything that for eighteen years had been dear and familiar.

He had given her, instead, a strange, unreal happiness for a short time.

He had made her believe mistakenly that he was the only thing she owned and if she lost him she would be completely and utterly alone.

That was indeed what had happened.

Secondly, like a meteor passing through the sky, had come the Marquis of Colthaust.

She had loved him with a passion that was quite different from the romantic emotions of the eighteen-year-old Rosamund Ormond.

But he had left her, and the agony of that loss could still keep her awake at night.

It made her in the daytime think she would prefer death to anything else.

Now he was here! Here! And she knew that he would be an old man

If she was fifty-six, he must be nearly seventy, and his son, as Amy had already told her, was following in his father's footsteps.

"They says as Lilly Layman's so infatuated with th' Viscount she finds it impossible when she gets on the stage to remember her lines."

"How do you know that?" Rosie asked.

"They was a-talkin' about it down at t'Gaiety," Amy replied. "That's the third girl he's had in love with him this year. They're all the same, they falls in love wiv his looks, his money, an' his honeyed tongue. A right 'chip off the old block'! That's wot he is!"

Because she knew Rosie was curious, Amy went to the Theatre more often than usual.

The newcomers who had taken Amy's place in the dressing-room were always glad to see her.

They would gossip over a pint of ale or, if one of the stars was generous, a glass of champagne.

Then Amy would come home, bursting to tell Rosie what was happening.

Nothing went on at the Gaiety that was not known by everybody.

Each girl vied with the others in having the most admirers.

They concentrated on those who would give them the best time, the most expensive jewelry, and the largest parties.

The Viscount Colt had been a law unto himself, just as his father had been.

He was not so much interested in parties as in conquering any one girl who had taken his fancy.

He captured her not because he was rich or important, but because he was such an attractive man that they could not resist him.

'Honey-tongued was the right description,' Rosie thought.

She remembered the things Lionel Colthaust had said to her.

Like a stupid little rabbit hypnotised by a snake, she had found it impossible to resist him.

She had the idea, based on the tales that Amy carried to her, that the Viscount would be attracted, as his father had been before him, by the girls who were young and beautiful in an unsophisticated way.

Rosie knew it was her fair hair, her blue eyes, and her child-like belief in love which had made her so attractive to him.

Then it had all been very natural because she had found the man who held her heart.

He enveloped her with such happiness and beauty that she could ignore anything around her that was unpleasant.

Only when the Marquis had left her did she realise how much she had lost.

The reality she had to face was hard, cruel, and even brutal.

Although her mind told her one thing, she still seemed to have her eyes filled with stars, though she had by then learnt not to express her real feelings.

Instead, she told a man what he wanted to hear.

That was inevitably something flattering about himself.

Young Rosie would never have thought out a plan of revenge on anybody.

Least of all on her family, or on the man she had once loved.

But the Rosie who had had to fight for herself and tell herself over and over again that nothing counted except money was a very different person.

Because she was acting out her own drama, it seemed as if Fate were on her side.

Everything she wanted would come true.

* * *

Viscount Colt was dining with a party at the Hôtel de Paris.

The huge Dining-Room was packed, and by nine o'clock it seemed as if there was not an empty chair in the whole room

And yet there was one table in the very best position near the window which was still empty.

It was not obvious because at every other table there were women glittering with diamonds and ospreys that caught the eye.

The gentlemen, elegant in their long-tailed evening coats and stiff white shirt-fronts, provided exactly the right background.

It was a glamour which could not be exceeded anywhere at this season of the year in the whole of Europe.

"I must say, Victor," Lord Charles remarked, "I have seldom seen so many beautiful women in one place, except of course on the stage of the Gaiety."

The Viscount laughed.

"I am inclined to agree with you, Charles," he replied, "but I am not yet certain whether the Gaiety is not more amusing individually, even though I have to admit that this collection is indeed exceptional."

His eyes rested for the moment on one of the most famous ballet-dancers from Russia.

Then he looked at an acknowledged Beauty who

was a member of the "Marlborough House Set."

At a table farther away was the mistress of the Grand Duke Alexis.

Her beauty was reported to have caused the suicide of at least three men once she was no longer interested in them.

Following his eye, Lord Charles laughed quietly.

Then he saw the expression on his friend's face as he turned to their own table.

It told him without words that the Viscount's present *affaire* was nearing its end.

The woman whom he had brought to Monte Carlo and who was staying with him at his father's Villa was very lovely.

At thirty-five, Lady Constance Fane had buried one husband and run away from her second to be with the Viscount.

She was five years older than he was.

It was, however, impossible to imagine any woman who could be more beautiful or more sophisticated in the art of attracting a man.

"What Constance does not know of the *'Science d'Amour,'*" somebody had said recently, "could be written on a postage-stamp!"

Because the man to whom that observation was addressed was aware that the Viscount was in the room, he said in a low voice to his friend who had made it:

"I think, of the two, I would back Colt, who is as knowledgeable on the subject of women as his father was, and that is saying a great deal!"

Lord Charles was now wondering where the Viscount's vacillating heart would beat next.

He was well aware that the Marquis, who was tied to the Villa with a gouty leg, had been known for years as "The Wicked Marquis."

There was no doubt that now his son, Victor, was

emulating his parent's reputation and even at times exceeding it.

"The Pursuit of Beauty!" Lord Charles said to himself.

He wondered if Lady Constance knew her reign was coming to an end.

He watched her now as she put her hand on the Viscount's arm to attract his attention.

"What are you thinking about, Victor?" she asked.

She spoke in a soft, seductive voice that made every word sound like a caress.

"I was thinking that you are undoubtedly the most beautiful woman present," he replied.

It was the answer she expected.

But Lord Charles, as he listened, thought the whole reply was too smooth, too automatic, as if the Viscount had said it without even thinking it.

As he spoke, people turned their heads as some latecomers were escorted across the room to the empty table by the window.

It was the table next to that occupied by Lord Charles and the Viscount.

Both men looked with interest at the very dignified elderly woman who walked across the room with a grace that made her seem like a sailing ship moving before the wind.

Both men asked themselves as they looked at her where they had seen her before.

Her face was familiar, but for the moment they could not put a name to it.

Then immediately behind her walked a girl.

She looked like Persephone herself coming out of the darkness of Hades.

She was very fair, a typical English beauty, but in some way she was different from the usual mould.

Her large eyes, which were the blue of the Mediterranean, seemed to fill her small, pointed face.

Her hair, which was arranged very simply, was the gold of the sunshine.

In it was just one pink rose which was not yet in full bloom. It was the only touch of colour, for her gown was white.

Yet again there was a difference from the white worn by the other young girls.

It shimmered with silver, it sparkled as if a dew-drop had fallen on a flower.

Then she was seated at the next table to the Viscount and Lord Charles, who stared at her because it was impossible to look away.

"Who is she?" Lord Charles asked as if he could no longer contain his curiosity.

"I have not the slightest idea!" the Viscount replied. "But she is the most beautiful creature on whom I have ever set my eyes!"

As he spoke, he noticed that the *Maître d'Hôtel* was moving away from the table to which he had escorted the latecomers.

He beckoned him to his side.

"Who are the ladies who have just arrived?" he asked in perfect French.

"They are Lady Rosamund Ormond, Milord, whom His Lordship your father'll remember was the star of the Gaiety Theatre, *Madame* Rosie Rill, and her niece, Miss Ina Wescott."

"Rosie Rill? I do not believe it!" the Viscount said beneath his breath.

Then as the *Maître d'Hôtel* moved away he said to Lord Charles:

"Surely the man is mistaken? He cannot really mean Rosie Rill?"

"Now you speak of it, I think I recognise her," Lord Charles replied. "I saw her only once before I went to Eton, but now I am sure it is her."

"And that is her niece!" the Viscount said as if he were reassuring himself that she was real.

It was then that Lady Constance, as if she must capture the Viscount's attention, said softly:

"Dearest Victor, you are neglecting me!"

"How can you think that possible?" the Viscount asked.

As he spoke, as if he were unable to prevent himself, he looked again at the exquisite, almost absurdly beautiful face of the girl sitting at the next table.

Lord Charles, doing the same, was aware that Lady Constance in comparison suddenly looked very old.

It must be just a trick of the light or perhaps it was because the newcomer was so obviously very young —too young to be in Monte Carlo.

Whatever her age, though, Lord Charles knew that she was unique in a way that he could not put into words.

What he did more clearly know was that as far as his friend the Viscount was concerned, Lady Constance was finished.

Although he had brought her with him to Monte Carlo, she would undoubtedly have to find somebody else to escort her home.

Because he felt sorry for her, Lord Charles began to talk to her animatedly.

They spoke of mutual friends he had found already since his arrival, and of others he expected to turn up before the end of the week.

"I am told it is the best season Monte has ever had," he said.

Then he saw that Lady Constance was not listening.

It was obvious to both of them that the Viscount had given up any pretence of being attentive to her.

He was just staring at Ina.

Rosie was well aware of the sensation their entrance had caused and of the interest that was being shown by the members of the next table.

But Ina was looking about her like a child who had suddenly stepped into Fairyland.

"I have never seen so many jewels, Aunt Rosamund!" she said. "And I did not know that women wore ospreys in their hair at night."

"They wear a great many more in the day!" Rosie replied. "They are a sign that the wearer is either very rich, or that the man with her can afford the best!"

She spoke without thinking, then realised it was the sort of thing she should not say to Ina.

Fortunately she was not really listening.

"Why does everybody come here?" she asked. "Is it that the food is better than anywhere else?"

"It is not the food that draws them so much as the company," Rosie explained. "The women who visit Monte Carlo want to see and be seen. It is a background for the rich, the successful, and the beautiful."

Ina laughed.

"Oh, Aunt Rosamund, you do say things in such a funny way! Somehow this does not seem real, but almost as if the people were taking part in a Play."

"That is exactly what they are doing," Rosie replied.

As she spoke she glanced at the next table.

She saw the expression on the Viscount's face as he looked at Ina.

I have been extremely clever! she told herself.

She had given the *Maître d'Hôtel* a huge tip to make sure that she was seated next to the table which had already been booked in the name of the Viscount Colt.

61

It had been worth every penny of it.

Now, unless she was very mistaken, the curtain was going up and the drama—her drama—was about to commence.

She gave a little sigh of satisfaction and ordered a half bottle of champagne for herself and some mineral water for Ina.

She did not ask her what she wanted, but ordered what she thought a young girl should be seen drinking.

In the same way, she had ordered gowns which she knew would make her *protegée* the focus of all eyes when they entered the Dining-Room.

"Youth," she said, "has an allure and a charm all of its own."

She remembered all too vividly how when she had first appeared on the stage there would be a little gasp from the men in the audience.

It was not only because she was very beautiful.

She personified an ideal which had always lain in their hearts, but which they had never expected to see.

'And what it cost me,' she thought cynically, 'was a brief time of enjoyment with two men, one of whom found money more attractive than love, and the other, blood.'

She turned again to look at the Viscount and felt she hated him because he was his father's son, and looked so like him.

Once Lord Colthaust had looked at her as his son was now looking at Ina.

Once he had talked to her in that low, deep voice, as if she were the only woman in the world, and held not only his eyes but his heart with her beauty.

For a moment she could feel again the agony she had known when he had left her.

The misery when she had gone down to the

Thames and felt the only way to end her suffering was to drown in its cold waters.

But she had not died. She had gone on living.

She had sworn that somehow, someday, she would make them realise—Lionel Colthaust, Vivian Vaughan, and her father—that she could not be defeated.

They were not strong enough, however hard they tried.

"I hate them! I hate everything they stand for, everything in which they believe, and everything they find important!"

She wanted to scream her defiance aloud so that the Viscount would hear it and tell his father that he was responsible for such an outburst.

Instead, she said something light and amusing to Ina, which made her laugh.

It was a very young, spontaneous sound.

It showed the dimples on either side of her mouth and seemed to make her eyes sparkle more brightly than they were already.

The Viscount was watching and Rosie was aware of it.

She remembered how his father had said that when she laughed it was the most attractive sound he had ever heard.

"They will not be laughing by the time I have finished with them!" Rosie vowed vindictively.

Then she drank a little of her champagne.

She felt as she did so that it helped her to plan exactly what she would do later in the evening.

chapter four

ROSIE deliberately lingered over dinner until the Dining-Room was half empty before she proceeded to the Casino.

She passed through the huge gaming-room with a disdainful expression on her face.

Following her, Ina stared excitedly at the *croupiers* sitting like sentinels at the end of each table.

The players were exactly what she expected they would look like.

The elderly women with huge hats trimmed with feathers.

Their greedy eyes intent only on watching the little white ball swinging round the roulette wheel.

The old men with claw-like hands clutching their counters.

The grandly-dressed women with dyed hair fawning on any man who had won.

The intonation of the *croupiers*, the cries of delight when somebody won, were all what Ina had imagined a Casino would be like, but even more dramatic.

Her aunt swept ahead of her towards the *Salle Privée* and was bowed in by liveried attendants.

Here the atmosphere was very different.

To begin with, it was much quieter.

The tables were not so crowded, and there were flowers, a soft carpet, and windows looking out into the night.

There was also the same sense of drama.

Yet, as Ina said to herself, a more aristocratic and controlled one.

Rosie moved slowly through the tables, ignoring the fact that there were several empty chairs at which she could have sat down.

She appeared to have eyes only for the gambling, but she was actually looking for one person.

When she saw him she stopped moving and stood staring at the table, hearing the *croupier* croon almost as if it were an incantation:

"Faites vos jeux, Mesdames et Messieurs."

The Viscount Colt was standing behind Lady Constance's chair.

She raised her lovely face to his to ask him on what number she should place her bet.

"I feel lucky tonight, Victor!" she said. "How could I be anything else when I am with you? What is your favourite number?"

The Viscount thought scornfully that every woman relied on signs and symbols rather than on her intuition.

He was well aware there were people in the Casino who believed that the most extraordinary things would influence the fall of the cards or the turn of the wheel.

There was one man who always carried salt in his pocket.

Another had a spider in a box and whichever way the spider moved would tell him whether to back *rouge* or *noir*.

There was a woman who believed fervently in a piece of rope by which a criminal had been hanged.

Another consulted a Gypsy every night before she came to the Casino.

The Viscount thought that such people were ridiculous in their superstitions and as boring as the games themselves.

He was not a gambler and, as he had only that evening said to Charles:

"A little of the Casino goes a long way with me. I have no intention of staying late."

"Quite right," Lord Charles replied. "After all, you have your amusements at home."

He looked at Lady Constance as he spoke, and following the direction of his eyes, the Viscount laughed.

He started to move away to find somebody to talk to, leaving Lady Constance inevitably to lose his money before she rejoined him.

A woman stumbled against him.

As she did so the plaques she held in her hand fell onto the carpet.

"I am sorry, I am so sorry!" Rosie exclaimed. "Somebody pushed me!"

"It is what inevitably happens in this place," the Viscount replied. "There are always people either hurrying to lose their money or, having done so, hurrying to commit suicide!"

Rosie laughed while Ina bent down to pick up the counters lying on the carpet.

The Viscount did the same.

He reached for the same counter as Ina did, and as he did so, he touched her fingers and they looked at each other.

She was so exquisite that for a moment he forgot

where they were or what he was doing.

He could only stare at her, feeling, as he had felt in the Dining-Room, that she was not real.

Then, because his eyes made her feel shy, she stood up.

He did the same, holding a counter between his thumb and forefinger.

He was still looking at Ina.

It was almost with a sense of shock that he heard Rosie say:

"I think that is the last counter I dropped, and thank you very much."

She took it from him as she spoke and put it with the rest in her other hand.

Then, as she would have turned away, the Viscount managed to say:

"May I introduce myself? I think you used to know my father—the Marquis of Colthaust. I have heard him speak of you."

"But of course!" Rosie said in pretended surprise. "I knew your father many years ago. Is he still alive?"

"Very much so," the Viscount replied, "but he had an attack of gout, which has confined him to the Villa."

"I am so sorry," Rosie said. "Gout, as we all know, is a very tiresome affliction."

"It is indeed," the Viscount agreed. "I know my father will be extremely interested to hear that you are in Monte Carlo."

Rosie inclined her head graciously.

Then, as it seemed as if once again she would move on, the Viscount said hastily:

"Is there anything I can do for you?"

He spoke to Rosie, but his eyes were on Ina.

Almost reluctantly, as if she thought it a mistake, Rosie replied:

"Perhaps I should introduce you to my niece, Ina

—this is the Viscount Colt, whose father I used to know a long time ago, when I was a little older than you are."

Ina smiled and it was as if the sun had suddenly illuminated the Casino.

She thought the Viscount standing in front of her was the most handsome man she had ever seen.

She put out her hand, and when he took it she felt as if there were something strong and what she could describe to herself only as a vibration from his fingers to hers.

She had taken off her gloves when they entered the *Salle Privée*.

Having lived in the country, she was not used to wearing gloves.

It had not, in fact, struck her that neither her aunt nor any of the other women present had removed theirs.

Now her hand was held by the Viscount, and when he looked down at her she had the feeling that his eyes were saying things that were more important than what he said with his lips.

"I am so delighted to meet you," he said in a low, deep voice. "When I saw you at dinner in the Hôtel de Paris I did not believe you were real!"

Ina gave a little laugh and replied:

"That is what I am thinking, and as I also feel none of this is real, I am only afraid I shall wake up."

Rosie gave an exclamation that seemed to intrude on the two people who stood beside her.

"I have a feeling I must play," she said.

Then, as if it was an afterthought, she said to the Viscount:

"Will you look after my niece for me for a few minutes? She has never been in a Casino before and I really should not leave her alone."

"Of course! I will be delighted," he replied.

There was an empty chair at the table a few seats away from where Lady Constance was sitting.

Rosie moved quickly towards it and sat down.

"Do you want to play?" the Viscount asked Ina.

"No, of course not," she replied, "and anyway, I have no money."

She spoke quite unselfconsciously.

He was aware, even without asking her, that it had never occurred to her for a moment to expect him, as Lady Constance did, to be her Banker.

"In that case," he said, "I would like to show you something which I think you would appreciate."

She looked up at him enquiringly.

Taking her arm, he led her through the crowds towards an anteroom, where people were drinking.

It contained a long French window that led out into the garden.

He opened the window, and as Ina walked out through it she had a glimpse of palm trees dark against the starlit sky.

They walked across the grass without speaking.

Suddenly she was aware that below them there were the lights of the harbour.

The yachts were reflected shimmering in the sea.

It was a very attractive scene when she had looked at it from her bedroom window while dressing for dinner.

Now that the stars were out and there was a new moon moving up the sky, it was lovelier than anything she had ever imagined.

At the same time, even more unreal.

She looked down at the harbour, then up at the sky, unaware that the Viscount was looking only at her.

After what seemed quite a long time, he asked:

"What are you thinking?"

Ina did not turn to look at him as he had expected.

Instead, with her eyes on the crescent moon she said:

"I was remembering my father saying once that when we see anything beautiful, hear an exquisite piece of music, or listen to a fine poem, it lifts the heart, and that in itself is a prayer."

She spoke almost as if she were speaking to herself.

The Viscount was aware that it was not for effect, but that she was truly translating her thoughts into words.

"So you were praying," he said softly, "and may I ask what for?"

"I was not asking for anything," Ina replied, "but thanking God because I am here and because I have been so unbelievably lucky."

She still did not turn her head towards him, and as if he wanted her attention he said:

"Come and sit down and tell me about it."

He moved her towards a seat that was set against a shrub in blossom and beneath the palm trees.

Obediently, almost like a child, Ina sat down.

The Viscount, turning towards her with his arm resting on the top of the seat, said:

"Now tell me about yourself."

"I would much rather talk of Monte Carlo," Ina answered. "I had heard so much about it, but I had no idea it could be so fantastic and at the same time so . . . different."

She made a little gesture with her hands as she said:

"That sounds contradictory . . . but that is what I feel . . . about it."

The Viscount thought with a faint twist of his lips that it was a very different conversation from those he usually had with women.

He was very well aware that he was more hand-some and certainly more distinguished-looking than any of his contemporaries.

He was used to women, whatever their age, finding him irresistible.

They threw themselves into his arms even before he asked them their names.

He had the strange feeling that this very young and beautiful girl was not thinking of him at all as a man.

Just as another dweller in a strange, bewildering place called "Monte Carlo."

"Have you lived with your aunt for some time?" he enquired.

Ina shook her head.

"Only for two weeks."

The Viscount looked puzzled.

It flashed through his mind that perhaps Rosie Rill had supplied herself with this young girl as a prop to attract attention.

Just as in India and Egypt the native beggar-women borrowed babies so that they could the more easily extort money from the visitors.

"You are making me curious," he said. "Why have you known your aunt, if she is your aunt, for only two weeks?"

"Of course she is my aunt!" Ina replied. "But I was never allowed to know her when Papa was alive. Then after he was dead, when I had no money and no idea how I could earn any, I went to London to ask Aunt Rosamund to help me."

She made it sound a very simple story, and yet the Viscount told himself he was not such a "greenhorn" as to believe it.

There was no possibility of Rosie Rill, lovely as

he had always heard she was when she was the star of the Gaiety, having a niece who was so breathtakingly beautiful.

There must be some out-of-the-ordinary explanation for it.

He could never remember Rosie Rill, whose name had been a household word when he was a Schoolboy, being Lady Rosamund, as she was calling herself now.

It was something he would certainly ask his father.

For the moment he was sure the whole thing was an act—a clever one, he admitted, but definitely an act.

It was obviously designed to attract a rich man like himself not for Rosie, who was far too old, but for her niece.

The *Maître d'Hôtel* had said that they had arrived only that day.

It struck him that, seeing how beautiful Ina was, the sooner he staked his claim, the better.

In fact, judging by the way Rosie had behaved, he did not think it would be difficult.

It was one of the oldest tricks in the world to drop money on the floor and wait for other people to pick it up.

It not only constituted an introduction.

In the past it had been one of the ways crooks in league with a dishonest *croupier* had managed to steal a great deal of money.

No, he thought to himself, Rosie would have to be cleverer than that to deceive him.

At the same time, there was no doubt that her accomplice was the most attractive girl he had ever seen in his life.

"How old are you?" he asked.

"I am eighteen."

"You are very young and very lovely," the Viscount said with just a touch of mockery in his voice, "and a lot of men must already have told you so."

"Not . . . where I have been . . . living," Ina replied.

"And where is that?"

"In my father's Vicarage in Redmarley in Gloucestershire."

She spoke so convincingly that the Viscount found it hard not to believe her.

Yet his intelligence warned him it was all too obvious, too contrived.

He felt he could almost write the story himself—a young and very beautiful girl comes to Monte Carlo for the first time.

She is bewildered by everything she sees, because previously she has lived in a Vicarage in the wilds of the English countryside.

She is introduced by her so-called aunt.

One of the famous stars of the Gaiety Theatre, whose name is still remembered with nostalgia, to a rich Viscount.

He had heard the servants talking about Rosie Rill when he was a boy.

Later his father's friends reminiscing about her and saying that the ambition of their lives had always been to take Rosie out to supper.

Because he was silent it made Ina think that perhaps she was doing something wrong.

She turned to look at him and said in a nervous little voice:

"I . . . I think we should . . . go back. Aunt Rosamund may be . . . looking for me."

"I can assure you," the Viscount said, "that as soon as somebody starts to play roulette or baccarat in the Casino, they forget everything else, and time has no meaning."

"I cannot believe Aunt Rosamund is . . . like that."

"And I cannot believe she is the exception to the rule," the Viscount said. "Everybody who comes to the Casino is caught like a foolish fly in a spider's web, and they gamble and gamble until all their money is gone."

Ina made a little cry of protest.

"That must not happen to Aunt Rosamund! We could not then afford to stay . . . here."

"In which case I shall invite you to come to stay with me," the Viscount said.

Ina laughed.

"That is unlikely, as you have only just met me! If we run out of money, I shall have to try to find some work . . . in . . . Monte Carlo."

"And what do you suggest you could do?" the Viscount asked.

Now there was a definitely cynical note in his voice.

He knew the answer, but he wondered if she would be brave enough to say it.

She did not speak for a moment, then she said:

"That was just what was worrying me when I went to see Aunt Rosamund. You see, both Papa and Mama were very anxious that I should be well-educated, but a little artistic talent and a little knowledge of the Classics do not equip one to earn enough money on which to live."

She paused for a moment and, as the Viscount did not speak, she went on:

"I have been thinking about this, and I somehow feel, although people may be shocked, that girls at school should be taught subjects which would qualify them, in case they become destitute, to find employment."

"And you were thinking there was nothing you could do?"

Ina made a helpless little gesture with her hands.

"I would like to be a Governess to small children, but I am . . . afraid people would think me . . . too young."

She sighed before she went on:

"I am sure Governesses are usually at least thirty before they are entrusted with the education of children who are old enough to leave the Nursery."

She shook her head.

"That would mean I would have to wait for a long time, and probably . . . starve in the process."

"You are painting a very sad picture of yourself," the Viscount remarked.

"I do not mean to do that," Ina said. "It is just that you frightened me by saying that Aunt Rosamund might lose all her money by gambling."

She paused.

"She has been so incredibly kind to me, and when I told her that she was spending too much, she said she could afford to give me beautiful clothes and take me to Monte Carlo because she had earned so much when she was on the stage."

"And off it!"

The Viscount with difficulty bit back the words and said instead:

"I suppose, seeing how successful your aunt has been, you did not contemplate going on the stage yourself?"

"No . . . I could not do . . . that," Ina said, "unless I was absolutely destitute."

Now there was a definitely frightened note in her voice.

"Why not?"

"Because it is something which would distress Papa very much."

"I thought you said your father was dead!" the Viscount remarked, thinking he had caught her out in her "hard luck" story.

"Yes, Papa is dead," Ina said in a low voice, "but of course wherever he . . . is he will know what I am doing. . . . And unless I was starving I would never do . . . anything which would . . . upset or . . . shock him."

The Viscount stared at her.

He was thinking that this was another way of "baiting the trap" which he had not encountered before.

Before he could say any more, Ina got to her feet, saying:

"I do not . . . want to seem rude . . . and thank you very much for showing me something so beautiful as the view from here . . . but I feel I should return . . . to Aunt Rosamund."

"Suppose I beg you to stay?"

He rose as he spoke and now he stood beside her.

"I would . . . like to stay because it is so . . . lovely out here," she answered, "but at the same time I must not do anything to . . . upset Aunt Rosamund after she has been so . . . kind to me. . . . I am sure you . . . understand."

"I will understand," the Viscount replied, "if you will say good-night to me."

She looked at him in surprise before she asked:

"Are you leaving?"

The Viscount moved a little closer to her.

"You were talking of leaving me."

She looked up at him, and as his arm went round her he said:

"What I am asking, Ina, is that you should let me kiss you good-night."

He was aware that for a moment she thought she had misunderstood what he said.

Then with a little cry she pushed him away, saying:

"No . . . of course not! That is . . . something you should not . . . ask me."

The Viscount caught her hand.

"But I have asked you," he said, "and I feel quite certain, Ina, that I would not be the first man to kiss you."

"Of course you . . . would be . . . if I . . . let you!" Ina replied. "I think it is . . . very wrong of you to ask . . . me."

She looked around the empty garden as if she were bewildered and then said:

"Perhaps it was . . . wrong for me to come . . . here with you in the . . . first place . . . . I think Mama would have been . . . cross with me for doing so."

She gave a little sigh and clasped her hands together.

"It is only that Monte Carlo seems so different so . . . please . . . please . . . will you . . . forget I came out into the garden . . . alone when I ought to have stayed . . . inside? And now I will go back . . . at once to Aunt Rosamund."

She moved away from him before he could stop her.

She had reached the glass door into the Casino by the time he caught up with her.

"I . . . I am . . . sorry," she said, "it was . . . all my fault . . . and perhaps Aunt Rosamund will be . . . angry with me."

There was anxiety in her large blue eyes and a trembling of her lips which the Viscount thought she could not have simulated.

Her appeal, her agitation, her embarrassment, and, most of all, her consternation in case she had done something wrong seemed very genuine.

Almost despite himself, he heard his voice say quietly:

"I am sure your aunt will not be aware that the

garden was empty except for ourselves, and I doubt if she will even have noticed your absence. If she has, I promise you I will make her understand that it was not your fault."

Ina's smile swept away her fear as she said:

"Thank you . . . that would be very . . . kind of you. Another time I will be more . . . careful. It was very . . . very . . . foolish of me not to . . . know how to . . . behave."

Before the Viscount could reassure her she had pushed open the door.

She was moving ahead of him back to the table where they had left Rosie.

She was still playing, and only as Ina reached her did she say:

"I have made a little money, but I think now, as we are both tired, we should have an early night."

"But of course, Aunt Rosamund."

Rosie got up from the table, and as if she were surprised to see the Viscount was standing there, she said:

"Thank you for looking after my niece. I do hope she has not bored you with too many questions. She has never been to Monte Carlo, or any other place like it before."

"That is what she has been telling me," the Viscount said. "I understand she comes from a Vicarage in Gloucestershire."

He watched Rosie as he spoke.

He was wondering if by a flicker of her eyes he would be able to guess that this was a lie.

They might have thought it up together to account for Ina's background.

Rosie hesitated for a moment before she replied:

"I never saw my youngest sister's home, so I am afraid all I know about it is what Ina has told me."

Before the Viscount could reply she held out her hand, saying:

"Good-night, My Lord, and thank you for your kindness. I am very grateful."

"It has been a pleasure," he replied.

Rosie started to walk away, and as she did so, Ina turned and held out her hand to the Viscount.

"Thank you," she said, "thank you very . . . very much, and I do not . . . think Aunt Rosamund is . . . angry with me."

"I am sure she is not," he answered, "and you must realise I want to see you tomorrow. Where can we meet?"

Ina looked surprised before she said:

"You will have to ask Aunt Rosamund."

"I want to see you alone."

Ina's eyes seemed almost to fill her face before she replied:

"That may not . . . be possible."

"Anything is possible if you want it enough, and I want it more than I have ever wanted anything before."

Ina laughed, and it was a very happy little sound and several people nearby turned to look at her.

"I do not believe that," she said, "and once again I think it is . . . something I should . . . not do."

"Is it your father or your mother who would disapprove this time?" the Viscount enquired.

Once again he could not keep the mocking note out of his voice.

Then he saw the colour rise in Ina's cheeks.

It made her look lovelier and at the same time more vulnerable than she did already.

"I think . . . you are . . . laughing at me," she said in a voice he could hardly hear.

Then quickly, like a small fawn that has been frightened, she took her hand from his.

She slipped away through the crowds to join Rosie before he could say any more.

He stared after her in bewilderment.

He saw her pass out through the door of the *Salle Privée* and disappear.

He had the strange feeling that he had lost something very precious.

*   *   *

Back in their Suite, Rosie was cross-examining Ina.

"What did the Viscount say to you?" she demanded.

"He...took me out into the garden to...see the stars, Aunt Rosamund...and the view of the harbour," Ina replied a little nervously. "Perhaps I... ought not to have gone...but when he said he had something to show me...I did not know what it was."

She looked at her aunt anxiously, and Rosie replied:

"I think everybody who comes to the Casino wants to see the view from the terraces. It is lovely in the daytime and even lovelier, I am told, at night."

Ina gave a little sigh of relief.

"It was only...after I had been there for some time...that I thought perhaps you might be... angry."

"What did you talk about?"

"The Viscount asked me where I came from, and when I told him it was from a Vicarage in Gloucestershire, he seemed to think it was rather... strange."

"And did he ask to see you again?"

"Y-yes...he said he wanted to see me again to-morrow."

"Where and at what time?"

There was a little pause before Ina answered, the colour coming into her cheeks.

"He said he wanted to see me...alone...but I was not sure if you would...allow me to do... that."

"The Viscount is a young man I would trust implicitly," Rosie said loftily. "Now, what are we doing in the morning? Let me see . . . I am sure we have not been invited to do anything important . . ."

Ina had no time to reply because Amy came into the room.

"I were half asleep when you rang for me," she said. "Now, hurry up and get to bed. You're not used to late nights, as you well know."

"I am enjoying them," Rosie argued. "I have lived too long to be treated as if I am still in the Nursery, but I am not yet ready for an Old People's Home!"

Amy laughed.

"I've been chatting to the chambermaids and they was saying as when you went downstairs you looked a real Lady to your fingertips."

"That is what I like to hear," Rosie said.

She saw Amy wanted to say something more to her, and she turned to Ina, saying:

"Hurry off to bed. There are a lot of things to do tomorrow, and I would not want you to look tired. Good-night child."

"I am not tired, Aunt Rosamund, only excited," Ina replied. "I will say a very special prayer of thanks to God tonight because you have been so kind to me and brought me to this wonderful . . . exciting place!"

She bent to kiss Rosie as she spoke.

Then, saying over her shoulder: "Good-night, Amy," she went from the room and across the darkened Sitting-Room into her own bedroom.

"She was a success!" Rosie said to Amy. "A great success!"

"How could she be anything else when she looks just like you when I first sees you?" Amy asked.

"She may look like me," Rosie said almost beneath her breath, "but she is going to be far more intelligent than I was. She is going to make sure, or I am for her, that her beauty gets her everything she deserves and a great deal more besides!"

"I believe you," Amy said, "tho' thousands wouldn't!"

She helped Rosie into bed.

Lying in the dark, Rosie thought with satisfaction that everything was going according to plan.

She knew exactly what she wanted for Ina—a future which would not be dominated as hers had been by the need for money.

Or the constant fear that what she had got might disappear overnight and leave her penniless.

"At the same time," Rosie said to herself in the darkness, "I will show them I am not easily defeated, and they will pay—pay for the way they treated me. I only hope it hurts them as much as they hurt me!"

Her one regret was that Vivian would not know about it.

Vivian was dead, but the Marquis was alive and so was her father, and they were the two men who would squirm at what she intended to do.

Squirm and be ashamed, embarrassed, and above all infuriated.

There would be nothing they could do, nothing they could say to prevent her from carrying out her revenge.

She gave a little chuckle in the darkness.

Finally, with a smile of satisfaction on her lips, Rosie Rill fell asleep.

* * *

In the room on the other side of the Sitting-Room, Ina was awake.

It was difficult to sleep when everything had been so exciting, and she kept seeing pictures in colour passing in front of her eyes of what had happened since they had left London.

The sleeper-train in itself had been a delight.

When she had stepped out of it into the sunlight to see everything more brilliant, more colourful, and brighter than anything she had ever known, her whole life had changed.

She was starting out on a voyage of discovery.

It was exciting and thrilling, and at the same time rather frightening.

Then, as in a kaleidoscope, she could see the diners in the beautifully decorated high-ceilinged Dining-Room.

She also saw the enormous Casino with its paintings on the walls, its lights illuminating the people as they sat at the roulette-tables.

But one face seemed to zoom out at her and one pair of eyes held hers captive.

Never had she imagined that any man could look so handsome and at the same time so aloof and autocratic as the Viscount.

Her father had been good-looking, but there was something kind and compassionate about him which made his eyes very different from those of the Viscount.

He had looked at her in a way which made her heart flutter in her breast.

Then in a strange manner, when they were sitting side by side in the garden, she had found, although it seemed absurd, that it was difficult to breathe.

It was all mixed up with the stars, the moonlight, the palm trees silhouetted against the sky.

Also the lights in the harbour shimmering on the water.

"Perhaps it is because I am so . . . ignorant about men," Ina told herself, "and that is why I . . . feel he is . . . different."

Yet she knew he was different.

Although she had been frightened when he said he

wanted to kiss her, she could not help feeling, now that she was alone, that it had been foolish to run away from him.

Perhaps it would have been very wonderful if he *had* kissed her!

Her mother had once said to her:

"I hope one day, my darling, you will find somebody whom you will love with all your heart and who will love you in the same way."

She had smiled at her daughter before adding as if to illustrate what she had just said:

"That is what I feel about Papa, and he feels about me."

"And is that why you ran away with him, Mama?"

"Of course it was. I knew I could never love any other man as I love your father, and if I wanted to be happy — and everybody wants to be happy — I had to be with him."

"It is very, very romantic, Mama, and I hope that I shall find someone just like Papa and live happily ever afterwards."

"That is what I pray will happen, my darling."

But Ina thought in the darkness, the Viscount was not in the least like her father.

He was extremely handsome but, because she was perceptive, she was aware he had not the kindness in his eyes that her father had.

There was also something a little strange about the way he had questioned her.

She had the feeling he did not entirely believe her when she told him that she came from Gloucestershire.

He had also seemed doubtful as to whether her Aunt Rosamund was really her aunt.

'He must know some very odd people,' Ina thought.

Then, still seeing his face in the darkness, she

remembered how he had said he wanted to see her tomorrow, and—alone.

"I am sure it would be impossible," she told herself. "At the same time, I want to be with him, I want to talk to him, but if he asks me again if he can kiss me, I must of course say 'no.'"

Then again it flashed through her mind that it might be very wonderful if he put his arms around her and she could not escape from him.

She had the unmistakable feeling that she might vibrate to him in the same way as she had when he had taken her hand.

But she told herself firmly that she must behave in a proper and ladylike manner as her mother would have expected her to do.

She was sure that men and women should not kiss each other unless they were really in love and engaged to be married.

"If he were really in love with me," Ina reasoned, "to kiss him would be the most glorious and perfect thing that could ever happen."

Then she stopped.

"But if he is treating me as a pretty child, or as a fast woman, that would be . . . horrible!"

She suddenly had the idea that perhaps because of her aunt's profession, the Viscount might think she, too, was like a Gaiety Girl.

They went out to supper alone with gentlemen and kissed actors when they were on the stage.

She wondered if that was why her father disapproved of actresses.

Why her mother never spoke of her sister, unless they were alone together.

Looking back into the past, Ina could remember saying once to her mother:

"Why do none of your relatives ever come to visit you, Mama? Grandpapa may have been angry when you ran away from home, and I suppose the rest of the family who lived at home had to do what he wanted."

She looked at her mother searchingly.

"But your sister Rosamund also ran away, so you have something in common."

She realised her mother had hesitated before she replied:

"I think your Papa, being a Parson, does not approve of people who are on the stage."

"Why not?"

Her mother had found it difficult to explain.

It was, she said finally, not considered respectable to exhibit oneself so that ordinary people could pay to see on the stage someone who was what the servants called: "gentle-born."

"Do you mean that a Lady should not act, because people are able to pay to watch her?"

"Exactly!" her mother said.

"But surely it does not make your sister wicked, Mama, like the people Papa talks about in his sermons, who will not come to Church?"

"It is rather different from that," her mother had replied. "At the same time, darling, as it would upset your father, you must not talk about the Gaiety Theatre when he is listening."

She smiled at Ina.

"As you are never likely to meet an actress or know anything about them, there is no point in discussing them with him."

Ina had been aware that her mother was talking very earnestly.

Now she thought that perhaps because Aunt Rosamund had been kissed when she was playing a part on the stage, men would try to kiss her off the stage.

And that was why the Viscount wanted to kiss her.

"It is something I must not let him do," she told herself firmly, "and if I am alone with him, I must behave very . . . very . . . properly, just as Papa would want . . . me to."

But she had the feeling that it was going to be difficult.

There was something demanding, strong, and very virile about the Viscount.

Something that made her suspect it would be difficult to persuade him not to do something he wished to do.

However, she was not really afraid of him.

She wanted, if she was honest, to see him again and to talk to him and listen to his deep voice telling her how lovely she was.

"It is very . . . very exciting being here . . . God," she whispered before she fell asleep, "but will You please . . . help me to behave as Papa would . . . want me to . . . however difficult it . . . may be?"

Her eyes were closed, before she murmured a quiet: "Amen."

Then almost before the word left her lips she was asleep.

chapter five

INA woke early and because she was so excited she jumped out of bed and ran to look out of the window.

The sun was just breaking through the haze that lay over the sea.

It gave an ethereal impression that made everything seem unreal and part of a dream.

Amy brought Ina her breakfast, saying as she did so:

"Now there's no hurry for you, an' I wants Miss Rosie to sleep late. She's not used to gettin' to bed after midnight."

Ina laughed.

"Was it really as late as that?"

"It was!" Amy said in an uncompromising tone of voice.

Having eaten what she thought was a delicious breakfast of hot *croissants,* coffee, and fruit, Ina dressed herself.

She put on one of the pretty morning-gowns that Rosie had bought for her in Bond Street.

It was so lovely that she was almost afraid to wear it.

But she could not resist the thought that perhaps the Viscount would admire her in it.

She was dressed and had arranged her hair in the same way that the expensive hairdresser sent up by the Hôtel had done it last night before Rosie took her down to dinner.

She thought, when she looked in the mirror, that she had been rather clever.

Then, as if that were a waste of time, she went again to the window.

Now the mist over the sea had almost dispersed.

The Mediterranean was not the deep blue it would become later in the day but the soft silver blue of the morning.

There was a knock on the door and Ina answered it.

There was a page holding out for her a large basket of orchids.

"For you, *Ma'mselle*," he said in French.

"There must be some mistake . . ." Ina started to say.

Then saw her name was written on an envelope which was tucked into the basket.

The handwriting was strong and upright, and with a leap of her heart she felt sure she knew who had sent it.

"Merci beaucoup," she said, "but I am afraid I have nothing to give you."

"That's all right, *Ma'mselle*," the page replied, "the gentleman looked after me."

He grinned at her.

There was an expression in his eyes which told Ina that, young though he was, he admired her.

She took the basket into her bedroom, looking at it with awe.

She had never imagined she would ever receive anything so extravagant and exciting as a basket of orchids.

She opened the note and read:

> *Thank you for being so beautiful, and I am waiting downstairs to see you. Please do not disappoint me.*

C.

She read the note several times before she looked again at the orchids.

She thought how lovely they were and how fortunate she was to receive anything so beautiful.

Then she realised he was waiting downstairs and she was not certain what she should do about it.

She opened the door into the Sitting-Room.

Amy was there arranging some of Rosie's possessions on the writing-desk.

"Is Aunt Rosamund awake yet?" she asked.

"No, she ain't," Amy replied, "and don't you go wakin' her up."

Ina hesitated.

"I . . . I do not know what to do."

"About what?" Amy enquired.

"Viscount Colt has sent me a marvellous basket of orchids, and he says he is waiting downstairs. Do you think it would be all right for me to go down and thank him?"

"I'd think it'd be very rude if you didn't!" Amy replied.

"But what do you think Aunt Rosamund would say?"

"She'll be quite happy for you to be wiv him."

"If you are sure of that, then I will go down at once!" Ina said.

Her eyes were shining like stars, and without saying any more, she ran into her bedroom.

She did not put on her hat in case he would not wish to take her outside the Hôtel, but she carried it in her hand.

With a last look at the basket of orchids she set off down the corridor.

She was just about to descend the stairs to the second floor when a man came out of one of the rooms.

He joined her as she reached the top of the stairs.

"I saw you last night, Miss Wescott," he said. "and I hoped to have a chance to talk to you in the Casino, but you left early."

Ina looked at him and saw that he was a middle-aged man, tall, dark, impressive, and authoritative.

He had a way of speaking which prevented her from wondering if he should address her without an introduction.

"It was after midnight when we left," she said, "and that seemed very late to me!"

The man laughed before he said:

"We consider that early in Monte Carlo, but you do not seem curious as to why I was so eager to talk to you."

Ina looked at him in a puzzled manner, and he said:

"I wanted to tell you how beautiful you are and how much I admired your aunt when she embellished the stage at the Gaiety."

"I am sure Aunt Rosamund will be delighted that you remember her."

"As I am more than delighted to meet you."

There was something in the way he spoke that

made Ina feel a little uncomfortable.

As they were talking they had been slowly descending the staircase.

She wondered if it would seem very rude if she moved more quickly because she wanted to be with the Viscount.

"You are very lovely," the man said in a deep voice, "and perhaps I should introduce myself. I am the Grand Duke Ivor and I hope to entertain you in my Villa. I am sure, too, you would like to visit my yacht which is in the Harbour."

"Thank you," Ina said, "I will tell Aunt Rosamund of your kind invitation."

They had reached the last step of the stairs and were on the landing to the first floor.

The Grand Duke stopped, and standing in front of Ina, he said:

"The invitation is for you. I find you irresistible and more attractive than any woman I have seen for a long time. What I want, my little English Rose, is to make love to you."

He smiled in a sinister manner.

"I think it will be very exciting for us both."

Ina looked at him with astonishment.

Then, as he put out his hand to touch her, she gave a little cry of horror.

Slipping past him, she ran down the stairs as quickly as she could.

She was really frightened, not only by what the Grand Duke had said but also by something menacing and overpowering about him.

She felt, although she knew it was stupid of her, that she could not escape from him.

She was breathless by the time she reached the hall.

To her relief she saw standing in front of one of

the windows the broad shoulders and dark hair of the Viscount.

He had his back to her, but she felt she would have known him if there had been thousands of other men with him.

She ran across the hall and stood looking up at him.

"So you have come!" he said, as if he had been afraid she might refuse.

Then he asked:

"What is the matter? What has upset you?"

"There . . . was a . . . man . . . who talked to me on the . . . stairs," Ina gasped. "He said he was the . . . Grand Duke Ivor."

The Viscount frowned, then he said quickly:

"If you do not want to see him again, let us go out onto the terrace where we will not be disturbed."

Because Ina was frightened, she was prepared to do anything the Viscount suggested without arguing.

Still carrying her hat in her hand, she let him lead her down the steps of the Hôtel.

They crossed the road and went onto the terrace that lay at the back of the Casino.

There were a number of tables where people could sit to have an aperitif and also benches on the front of the terrace looking out over the sea.

It was too early for there to be many people about.

The Viscount led Ina to a wooden seat from which there was a magnificent view of the harbour, the Palace, and the sea beyond.

They sat down and he turned sideways to look at her.

He thought, with the sun shining on her hair and her worried blue eyes, deeper than the blue of the sea or the sky, she was not only very lovely but quite unusual.

"You are safe with me," he said, "but you are to have nothing to do with the Grand Duke—do you understand?"

"He . . . frightened me!" Ina said in a low voice.

"What did he say to you?"

The Viscount's question was sharp and he saw the colour rise in Ina's cheeks.

She looked away from him shyly before she answered:

"He . . . he said he wanted to . . . make love to me. Surely a . . . gentleman should not . . . speak to me like . . . that?"

The Viscount stared at her for a moment.

He thought she must be pretending, and that such a remark could not really alarm her.

Then he knew it would be impossible, however clever an actress she might be, to pretend to look so shocked and surprised, so agitated.

And at the same time to tremble as he knew she was, even though he was not touching her.

"You are very young," he said as if he spoke to himself.

"And very . . . ignorant of . . . people like that," Ina added.

"You were not impressed that he was a Grand Duke?"

"He was quite . . . old and said he had admired Aunt Rosamund when she was . . . on the stage . . . but the way he spoke to me did not . . . sound as if he were . . . reminiscing about the past."

She looked up at the Viscount.

Then as if she thought he was criticising her, she said with a little sob in her voice:

"I . . . I know you think I am . . . f-foolish in not behaving . . . as I . . . should . . . b-but I did not expect men to s-say that sort of . . . thing to me."

"It is something from which you must be pro-

94

tected in the future," the Viscount said, "and that is what I want to talk to you about, Ina, but not at this moment when you are so upset."

He smiled, then put out his hand and laid it on hers.

"Forget the Grand Duke," he said, "remember only that we are together and alone, just as I wanted us to be."

Ina felt as if she were suddenly safe and protected.

Then she felt as if her heart were turning over in her breast, because he was touching her.

"You are . . . right," she said, "and of course I must . . . forget him. Perhaps it was because he had too much to drink that he . . . said things like . . . that, but it does seem too early in the . . . morning for any-one to . . . drink anything but coffee."

The Viscount gave a little laugh, but he did not take his hand away from Ina's as she went on:

"Before I say any more . . . it was . . . very remiss of me not to . . . thank you at once for the . . . marvellous basket of orchids."

"They pleased you?"

"I have never seen orchids before, except in pic-tures, and they are even more beautiful than I ex-pected."

"And are they your favourite flowers?" the Vis-count asked with just a touch of cynicism in his voice.

Ina did not answer, and he added:

"I am sure they must be."

"It may seem . . . ungrateful when you have been so . . . kind and generous to me," Ina said hesitat-ingly, "but although the orchids are very, very lovely, in my opinion . . . the lily is more beautiful . . . and it is the . . . flower of God."

The Viscount studied her for a moment, then he said:

"If the orchids are not exactly what you would prefer, suppose we go shopping and I give you something you would like to possess more than anything else and something you chose yourself?"

"No . . . no . . . of course . . . not!" Ina said quickly. "You must think it very . . . ungrateful of me after you have been so kind, but you did ask me if orchids were my favourite flower . . . and I could not lie."

"No, of course not," the Viscount agreed, "and that is why I would like to give you a bracelet, or, if you prefer, a brooch, and we could find stones that are the colour of your eyes."

Ina stared at him in sheer astonishment before she said:

"Although it is . . . very kind of you to . . . think of such a thing . . . it is certainly . . . something I could not accept . . . and it would have been . . . far better if I had told . . . a lie about the orchids."

Her words seemed to fall over one another and the Viscount said:

"I would still have offered you a present of some jewelry, Ina. I noticed last night that you did not wear a necklace."

"I am sure Aunt Rosamund considers I am too young to borrow any of her jewels," Ina said, "or perhaps she thinks they are too precious and I might lose . . . them."

She paused to smile at him.

"In fact, she has already given me so many beautiful gowns that I do not want anything else."

"It is simply a question of what I would like to give you," the Viscount insisted.

"Please . . . I can only say again . . . thank you very . . . very much . . . but it is . . . something I cannot . . . accept."

"Why not?"

"Because I know it is incorrect . . . and also . . ."

Ina stopped speaking and made a helpless little

gesture with her hands.

Then she said in a puzzled voice:

"I cannot . . . understand why you should . . . want to give me . . . things when we have only . . . just met."

"I can answer that question quite easily," the Viscount replied. "I find you very adorable and lovely, and I have no wish to lose you."

Ina looked at him in perplexity, before with an uncertain little laugh she said:

"How can you lose me . . . when I do not . . . belong to you?"

The Viscount was just about to answer this when he thought it might be premature.

If he were as frank as he wanted to be, and if Ina were genuine, which he still somewhat doubted, he would frighten her.

He could hardly believe, however, that anyone who purported to be the niece of Rosie Rill could be so innocent and ignorant of men.

At the same time, Ina really did seem to be behaving as perfectly naturally as a girl would who, as she had told him, had come from the country only two weeks before.

Then, thinking again that her professed fear of the Grand Duke and refusal to accept a present from him might be all part of an act, he said to change the subject:

"If you do not wish to come shopping with me, which is something I have found most women enjoy in Monte Carlo, then what would you like to do?"

There was just a little pause before Ina said:

"I know what I . . . really want to do . . . but I am afraid it would . . . bore you."

"I seldom allow myself to become bored," the Viscount replied, "and I am certain I could never be bored with you."

Ina gave a soft little laugh before she said:

"How can you possibly know that, considering you have known me for such a short time?"

"I not only make up my mind very quickly," the Viscount answered, "but I knew from the moment I saw you that you were different from anybody I have ever seen before."

He paused before continuing:

"Then when I touched your hand as we picked up the counters your aunt had dropped, we were linked together in a way it is impossible to explain."

Ina gave a little start and looked at him wide-eyed.

"Did you . . . feel that . . . too?"

"I thought you felt the same!" the Viscount said. "So, Ina, what are we going to do about it?"

"It is certainly . . . strange," she said as if she were following her own line of thought. "Perhaps we have . . . known each other in . . . other lives, as the Buddhists believe."

"I cannot believe your father, an English Parson, told you about the 'wheel of rebirth'!" the Viscount remarked.

"But he did!" Ina insisted. "He wanted me to understand that all religions are there to help mankind and to make people, because of their faith, spiritually better human beings."

There was a little pause, then Ina added:

"You asked me what I wanted to do. . . . I have been hoping while I am in Monte Carlo to be able to visit . . . the Chapel of Sainte Dévote."

The Viscount looked surprised. Then he said:

"Is that the Chapel of some Saint of whom I have never heard?"

"But you must have heard of Sainte Dévote. She is the Patron Saint of the Rock."

"Who told you that?"

"I knew about it a long time ago, when first I read

the newspapers about the Bishops condemning gambling at Monte Carlo."

She smiled at him.

"It was then that . . . Papa told me about Sainte Dévote, who landed here in A.D. three hundred."

"You are telling me something I have never heard before," the Viscount said, "and I have been coming to Monte Carlo for many years."

"Sainte Dévote lived in Corsica," Ina said, "and was assassinated after she became a Christian. The Priest who had converted her planned to take her body to Africa, but the ship was blown far off course."

She paused with a far-away look in her eye.

"In a dream he saw a white dove fly from the breast of the dead girl and settle in a narrow ravine."

Ina's voice was very soft, and she was not looking at the Viscount as she spoke but staring out to sea.

Almost as if she could see it happening again.

"When the Priest awoke," she went on, "he found the ship had landed on the beach at Monaco and before it, perched on a ravine, was a white dove!"

"So that is why you wish to go to the Chapel of Sainte Dévote," he said as Ina finished. "Of course, if that is what you want, I will be delighted to take you there."

She gave him a smile that seemed to light up her whole face as she asked:

"Would you really? But, please . . . will you find out . . . first if it is far away . . . because I must not stay with you . . . very long in case Aunt Rosamund wakes up and . . . wants me."

"We will have time," the Viscount said confidently.

They walked back to the road, where there was a line of open carriages for hire.

The Viscount helped Ina into one and she put on

her hat as if she were suddenly aware that she should have been wearing it before.

The Viscount told the coachman to take them to the Chapel of Sainte Dévote.

He thought as he did so that the *cocher* did not seem very pleased with the order.

He therefore was not surprised when just at the bottom of the hill the *voiture* turned right instead of left.

In the centre of what was obviously a high ravine they saw the Chapel which Ina wanted to visit.

The Viscount helped her out of the carriage.

She gave him a little smile before she walked up the steps of the Chapel and pushed open the baize-covered door.

It was a very small building, dim and cool inside, the light coming from the candles illuminating the Chancel.

There was nobody there except for two elderly women wearing black shawls over their heads.

Ina was instantly aware of an atmosphere which seemed to her redolent with the faith of ages.

Without really thinking of the Viscount, she moved into the first row of chairs at the back of the Chapel and knelt down.

He stood looking at her as she clasped her hands together and shut her eyes.

He thought it was a long time since he had seen a woman praying, and certainly not one who was so young and so beautiful.

He was certain there was no question of it being part of an act.

As he watched her, Ina opened her eyes and looked up at the altar with its sacristy lamp gleaming in front of it.

There was an expression on her face which the Viscount knew revealed what she felt.

They were feelings that came from her heart, or perhaps the right word was her "soul."

What he was seeing could never have been contrived artificially by any actor or actress, however brilliant, however gifted.

Ina prayed for about two minutes, then she rose from her knees.

Walking back to the way they had entered the Chancel, she turned to genuflect to the altar.

The Viscount opened the door for her and they went outside.

Only as they went down the steps and he helped her back into the carriage did she say:

"Thank you . . . thank you for taking me there! It was just as I felt it would be."

She paused, and continued a little breathlessly:

"It was almost as if I stepped back . . . in time and could . . . feel the excitement of . . . the Priest when he saw . . . the white dove and knew this was . . . where he should bury the . . . body of Sainte Dévote."

There was a rapturous note in her voice.

The Viscount could not help thinking that the women he had known in the past had spoken in such a way only when they were eulogising over him personally.

Certainly not over an obscure Saint who had been dead for many hundreds of years.

"And now what would you like to do?" he asked.

"I think . . . perhaps I ought to . . . go back to Aunt Rosamund."

"Are you really in such a hurry to leave me?"

"It is not that," Ina said, "I love being with you, and I love talking to you. You have also been very kind to me . . . but I do not want to do anything . . . wrong."

"I am sure your aunt would not feel it wrong for you to be with me," the Viscount said, "and the morning is still young, Ina."

"I have been awake for a long time."

"So have I," he replied, "and because I wanted to see you, I did not go riding as I usually do, but came into Monte Carlo to find the orchids, which I hoped would please you."

Ina drew in her breath and her eyes, as she looked at him, were very expressive.

"We have a lot to talk about, Ina," the Viscount said very quietly as the carriage came to a stop outside the Hôtel de Paris.

"Anywhere else you wish to go, *Monsieur?*" the *Cocher* enquired.

The Viscount got out and paid him, then he put his hand under Ina's arm and once again guided her across the road to the terraces.

Now there were more people about than there had been before, but the seat where they had sat was empty.

He led her towards it.

They sat down side by side and she looked at him enquiringly.

"You know I want to be with you," he said. "What I suggest is that you go back to the Hôtel and ask your aunt if I can take you out to luncheon."

He smiled at her.

"I will drive you up to La Turbie, where you can see the pillars built by the Romans when they were here and have a fine view of the whole coast."

"I would love that," Ina said, and he knew there was no pretence in the way she spoke.

"Then that is what we will do," he said, "and I will escort you to your Suite, so that you will not be bothered by Grand Dukes or anybody else until I can see you again."

"Please . . . do . . . that," Ina begged.

She would have risen to her feet, but the Viscount did not move.

"You are so beautiful," he said, "so unbelievably beautiful that I do not think you are real."

He took her hand in his as he spoke and said:

"If you want to be with me as much as I want to be with you, we will be very happy."

He felt her fingers quiver in his before she said:

"But . . . of course I . . . want to be . . . with you. You have been so . . . wonderful in taking me to . . . the Chapel, and I would rather have . . . gone there with . . . you than . . . anybody else."

"Why do you say that?" the Viscount asked.

She hesitated a moment before she replied:

"I may be wrong . . . but I feel you . . . understood as . . . nobody else would . . . have."

She paused again, then she said almost in a whisper:

"I do not think that . . . Aunt Rosamund is . . . very religious and she seemed . . . surprised when I went to . . . Church last . . . Sunday. She sent Amy with me, but she did not . . . go herself."

"So you did not think she would be interested in coming with you to the Chapel of Sainte Dévote?"

Ina's eyes flickered and she looked a little embarrassed before she said:

"I . . . I thought she might . . . laugh at me for wanting to . . . do that."

"Yet you thought I would understand."

"You . . . did understand . . . and you took me . . . there."

Now she was looking up at him with an expression of trust in her eyes which the Viscount found somewhat perturbing.

It was with an effort that he said:

"I want to look after you and protect you from anything which could upset you, and that is something we can talk about at luncheon."

"I do hope I shall be . . . able to accept your invitation."

103

"Then let us go and find out."

They rose and walked back to the Hôtel.

As they entered the hall, which now seemed to be filled with people, a lady, beautifully dressed and wearing a hat covered in ospreys, gave a cry of delight.

"Victor! It is you!" she exclaimed. "I thought I should see you here!"

The Viscount bent over her hand before he said:

"It is delightful to meet you again, Belle. You always make Monte Carlo more glamorous and, of course, more fascinating than it is without you."

Looking at the Viscount's friend, Ina had never imagined a woman could be so beautiful or look so glamorous.

Not only was her hat with its ospreys fantastic, but so was her gown.

It had sleeves ending at the elbow and tier upon tier of black lace falling to the floor.

Round her neck were five rows of huge, perfect pearls.

The Viscount made no attempt to introduce Ina to his friend, which she thought was strange.

Then, as they moved away, the Viscount, having once again kissed the lady's hand, Ina asked when they were out of ear-shot:

"Who was that . . . lovely lady?"

"That is *La* Belle Otero."

"She is very beautiful!"

"And very, very expensive," the Viscount said without thinking, "as a large number of gentlemen have found to their cost."

"Expensive?" Ina questioned. "Is she an actress?"

He thought with a twist of his lips that Rosie Rill's niece could not be quite so ingenuous as not to understand what he implied.

Then he answered truthfully:

"Yes, she is a dancer."

"She must be . . . very successful to own such . . . beautiful pearls."

"Do you think she earned those by her dancing?" the Viscount enquired. "Is that, perhaps, something you could do?"

Ina laughed.

"Now you are teasing me again! I do not think anyone would pay me a penny for dancing for them, and if I did possess a lot of money, there would be a great many other things I would prefer to spend it on before I bought pearls."

"What sort of things?" the Viscount asked as they climbed the stairs.

He thought that now at last they were getting down to business.

Ina was silent for a moment, as if she were thinking before she said:

"There are people at home in the village whom I would like to help because they are very poor, and I know how much they will miss Papa and Mama, who did everything they could for them."

"And what would you buy for yourself?" the Viscount persisted.

"I would buy myself a dog that I could love and which would be a companion so that I would never feel lonely even without Mama and Papa," Ina answered. "Then if I were very extravagant and very rich, I would buy myself a horse."

It was not what the Viscount had expected her to say, and after a moment he asked:

"Are you telling me you want to ride?"

"I used to do so when I was at home," Ina replied, "but of course it would be different here in Monte Carlo, and even if I had a horse, I could hardly ask Aunt Rosamund, after she has done so much, to provide me with a habit!"

Then she laughed and said:

"It is just like that stupid rhyme:

For the want of a nail the shoe was lost,
For the want of a shoe the horse was lost,
For the want of a horse the battle was lost.

Do you remember learning that when you were a boy?"

The Viscount realised that yet again she had not told him what he could give her.

By now it was too late as they had reached the door of her aunt's Suite.

The key of the Sitting-Room door was in the lock and as Ina turned it she said:

"Ought I to ask you to . . . come in? Then my aunt can . . . speak to you if she . . . wants to do so."

"Is this your Sitting-Room?" the Viscount enquired.

Ina nodded.

"Then it is quite correct for you to do so," he said gently.

"Then please come in," she said. "I wanted to ask you, but I was not certain . . . that it was . . . correct."

They went into the Sitting-Room and Ina said:

"Will you please sit down and I will find out if Aunt Rosamund is awake."

She went across the room and opened the door into her aunt's bedroom very, very softly.

She was aware that the blinds had been drawn, so she went in, shutting the door behind her.

*   *   *

Alone in the Sitting-Room, the Viscount walked to the window.

He was thinking as he did so that while he was determined to have Ina to himself, it would not be as easy as he had anticipated.

106

Not that he was afraid Rosie Rill would be difficult, but Ina.

*　　*　　*

After she had finished her breakfast, Rosie was sitting up in bed wearing a very becoming dressing-jacket.

She was reading the newspaper.

She found with satisfaction that all three of those published in Monte Carlo had devoted quite a lot of space to her arrival at the Hôtel de Paris with her niece——the grand-daughter of the Earl of Ormond and Staverley.

She had awoken soon after Ina had gone downstairs and Amy, as soon as she had drawn back the curtains and put down her breakfast-tray, said:

"D'you want to see th' orchids His Nibs has had delivered to Miss Ina this mornin'?"

"Orchids?" Rosie queried. "Of course I want to see them!"

Amy fetched the basket from Ina's bedroom with the note.

Rosie hardly looked at the orchids, but she read the note through twice with a smile of satisfaction on her lips.

"This is exactly what I wanted!" she exclaimed.

"I thought you'd be pleased!" Amy remarked with a sharp note in her voice.

Rosie did not bother to reply.

She waited until Amy had left her, then opened a leather case which she had set down by her bed.

In it there were a number of letters tied up with ribbon.

She took one out of a pile of which there were at least thirty, and compared the hand-writing with the note Ina had received from the Viscount.

There was a slight difference, but it was not particularly obvious unless one was specially looking for it.

What was more, the letters that Rosie had were all signed in the same way as Ina's note, with a "C."

Without really meaning to do so, Rosie read the note that she had received from the Marquis nearly twenty years ago . . .

> *My darling—*
>
> *I shall be late tonight, but do not worry. I shall turn up in the early hours, when I hope to find you asleep.*
>
> *You were more adorable last night than I can possibly tell you, but I shall try to do so tonight, however late it may be.*
>
> C.

There was a hard expression in Rosie's eyes as she finished reading the letter. Putting it back into its envelope, she tied it up with the rest.

Then she lay back against her pillows with Ina's note from the Viscount lying in front of her, and a smile curved her lips.

chapter six

WHEN Ina entered Rosie's bedroom she found her sitting in front of the mirror making up her face.

Since she had become Lady Rosamund again, this was a delicate operation.

Very different from the days when she had slapped on the rouge and powder because it had become a habit with her.

Now just a faint powdering on the nose, a touch of pale pink on her lips, and a little grease on her eye-lashes instead of mascara was all she allowed herself.

She turned her head to smile at Ina as she came towards her.

She was looking, Rosie thought, very attractive in one of the new gowns she had bought for her in Bond Street.

"Aunt Rosamund . . . I have . . . something to . . . ask you," Ina said in a breathless little voice.

"What is it, my dear?" Rosie enquired.

"The Viscount has asked me if I will have . . .
luncheon with him and has offered to drive me up to
La Turbie so that I can see the . . . Roman pillars and
the . . . view of the coast."

She paused, then added quickly:

"But only if you will not feel lonely without me
and . . . then of course I will stay with you."

Rosie smiled at her own reflection in the mirror.

"That is very thoughtful of you, my dear, but of
course you must go with the Viscount. What he has
suggested sounds a delightful thing to do."

"You will be . . . all right on your . . . own?" Ina
persisted.

Rosie thought of the long years she had been
alone in her flat in London.

What was important was that her plan was working out exactly as she wanted.

"As it happens," she replied, "I am feeling rather
tired, and have a slight headache, so it will be an
opportunity for me to eat in my Sitting-Room and
rest afterwards."

"Then . . . I may . . . go?"

Rosie did not miss the little note of excitement in
Ina's voice.

"Yes dear, and tell the Viscount to take great care
of you. You are very precious to me."

Ina hesitated.

"He is next door if you would like to speak to
him."

Rosie was just about to say that she would, when
she realised that she was only half-dressed.

She was wearing a negligée, and she knew it
would certainly shock Ina if she received the Viscount without being fully gowned.

"You can give him the good news yourself," she
said quietly. "He must be very attentive to have come
upstairs with you."

Ina looked embarrassed, then she said:

"I . . . I was frightened by . . . a man on my way down."

"A man?" Rosie asked sharply. "Who was it?"

"He said he was the . . . Grand Duke Ivor and he came out of a room on the second floor."

"Where he had been visiting *La* Belle Otero!" Rosie said as if to herself.

Ina remembered that *La* Belle Otero was the beautiful lady who had spoken to the Viscount.

"What did the Grand Duke say to you?"

"He said he would . . . invite me to . . . stay in his Villa and to . . . visit his yacht."

Ina paused before she continued in a small voice:

"Then he said some . . . very strange things which frightened . . . me and made me . . . run away."

Rosie's lips tightened.

"You are to have nothing to do with the Grand Duke!" she insisted. "He has a reputation for pursuing every pretty face he sees while his poor wife is left in Russia with their children."

"Do you mean to say that . . . the Grand Duke is a . . . married man?"

Ina gasped.

"Of course he is," Rosie replied.

Then she was aware that Ina was even more shocked to think it was a married man who had made such suggestions to her.

"Forget him!" Rosie said sharply. "Concentrate on the Viscount. He is a charming young man and comes from a most distinguished family."

"He is . . . very kind to . . . me."

Ina bent forward as she spoke to kiss her aunt's cheek and say:

"Thank you, Aunt Rosamund, for giving me such a . . . wonderful time, and I will tell you all about . . . my visit to La Turbie when I get . . . back."

"I shall be looking forward to hearing all about it!" Rosie smiled.

Ina almost ran across the room, eager to be with the Viscount again, and Rosie sat staring with unseeing eyes at her own reflection.

It seemed incredible that everything was working out exactly as she had imagined it might before she left London.

She had been sure that the Viscount would be, as Amy had told her, a "chip off the old block."

He would be fascinated by someone so young and fresh as Ina, just as his father had been where she was concerned.

But now she had the "whip hand."

As soon as the Viscount discarded Ina, which he would inevitably do in the same way that she had been discarded, she would sue him for Breach of Promise.

The newspapers would make it a *cause célèbre*.

Already he was writing notes to Ina, and she was sure there would be a great many more.

She intended also to assert that his father's affectionate letters to her were also from him.

It would be difficult for him to disprove the accusation.

The Marquis would have to go into the witness-box himself to prove who had actually written them.

She could see all too clearly the headlines that would be carried by the newspapers.

She knew the way they would emphasise the Marquis's importance in the Social World.

Also her father's as Lord Lieutenant of Hertfordshire.

The scandal would reverberate over the whole of England.

Rosie knew only too well how both her father and the Marquis would hate every word that was written about them.

There would be photographs of Ina looking lovely, and photographs of herself at the height of her fame.

There would also be photographs of the Viscount and his father, as both were exceedingly handsome men.

Only when she had dragged the reputation of her own family and theirs into the dust would she feel satisfied.

She was confident that the compensation they would have to pay Ina would be very large.

What was more, since the girl would be the "Injured Party," Rosie could well imagine how women of all classes who read the newspapers would sympathise.

They would be appalled that anyone so young and lovely had been betrayed by an experienced Don Juan.

She stayed in her bedroom until Amy told her that the Viscount and Ina had left the Sitting-Room.

Then, wearing one of her distinguished gowns and an attractive hat trimmed with feathers, she went downstairs.

As she reached the hall the Grand Duke Ivor, who was sitting with several friends, rose to his feet and came towards her.

"Good-morning, Rosie Rill!" he said. "I want to talk to you."

Rosie dropped him such a small curtsy that it was almost an insult before she said:

"My name, Your Royal Highness, is Lady Rosamund Ormond."

"I am aware of that," he replied, "at the same time, as you know, I have admired you for many years, and we met at a number of parties."

He had a twisted smile on his lips as he continued:

"You were the most beautiful of all the stars who graced the Gaiety."

"You flatter me," Rosie said in a voice that did not sound as if she appreciated his compliment.

"Come and sit down for a moment," he said, "I have something to say to you."

There were two empty chairs in the corner of the hall.

As she sat down, Rosie thought that despite the fact that he was a middle-aged man, the Grand Duke had worn well and looked very distinguished.

If things had been different, she might, in fact, have considered what he was about to say to her.

She knew that to the Russian Grand Dukes money was plentiful and they spent it lavishly.

However, the plan she had worked out for Ina must on no account be interfered with.

So her back was straight and there was a hard expression in her eyes as the Grand Duke said beguilingly:

"I am infatuated, completely and absolutely infatuated, Rosie, with your niece. After you, she is the loveliest thing I have ever seen."

Rosie did not answer and he went on:

"I am prepared to look after her for you and make certain she has everything any woman could want."

He stopped to look at her.

"Jewels, furs, horses, and, of course, a house in Paris which will be hers with the deeds deposited in her Bank."

He finished speaking and Rosie looked down at her hands almost as if she were considering what he was offering.

Then slowly she rose to her feet.

"I regret having to disappoint Your Royal Highness," she said, "but you cannot offer Ina something which is far more precious and, to her, very much more valuable."

"What is that?" the Grand Duke asked.

"A wedding ring!"

She saw the astonishment on his face before she dropped him a perfunctory curtsy and, turning, walked away.

She went out through the front door while he stared after her in sheer bewilderment.

She crossed the road and went onto the terrace as Ina had done earlier with the Viscount.

Now sitting at most of the tables were elegant women and well-dressed gentlemen sipping aperitifs.

Rosie moved to an empty table at the far end of the terrace and sat down.

A waiter quickly appeared at her side to ask for her order, but before she could speak, a voice from the table next to hers said:

"May I have the privilege and honour of offering you a glass of champagne?"

She turned her head and saw sitting just behind her was a man in a wheel-chair.

His hair was going grey, but he was good-looking in his own way, quite obviously a gentleman and English.

"Have we met?" Rosie enquired.

"I have known you for a great number of years," was the reply, "and I would like to tell you about it."

Because she was interested and also because it was a change from being alone, Rosie rose.

She moved to the table beside the man in the wheel-chair, and sat down.

He ordered a bottle of champagne from the waiter and when the man had left said to Rosie:

"I can hardly believe my luck! All my life I have dreamt of talking to you and telling you how much you have always meant to me, and now, almost like a miracle, you are here!"

Rosie laughed.

"You make it sound very dramatic!"

"It is, to me," he said quietly.

Rosie glanced down at his legs covered with a light rug and he explained:

"I broke my leg out hunting and it has taken an inordinate amount of time to mend. Then my doctors decided I was run down, and advised me to come here to recuperate."

He paused.

"But nothing could be more effective in bringing about a cure than meeting you!"

Rosie could not help instinctively reverting to what she had been in the past, and looked at him almost flirtatiously as she said:

"Thank you! But tell me why you claim to have known me for so long."

"It is difficult to explain what you have meant to me in my life," the man replied. "First, I should introduce myself. I am Sir Stephen Hardcastle. I inherited my father's baronetcy three years ago."

Rosie smiled but she did not interrupt, and he went on:

"It was very unexpected and the result of losing both my elder brothers. One was killed on the North-West Frontier in India, the other fighting with General Gordon in Khartoum."

"I cannot bear to think of that siege," Rosie said in a low voice. "General Gordon was indeed a hero."

"When I first saw you," Stephen Hardcastle went on as if she had not spoken, "I was a young Subaltern of twenty-three."

He smiled at her.

"I was drawn to the Gaiety like all young men because it meant glamour, laughter, excitement, and, of course, the most lovely girls in the world."

He looked at Rosie and she thought he was seeing her not as she was now, but as she had been then as he added:

"The most beautiful of them all, of course, was you!"

"I suppose," Stephen Hardcastle went on, "I fell in love with you the moment you stepped out onto the stage."

He gave a sigh.

"When I went back to India, no other woman I met could compare with your sweetness or the inexpressible loveliness of your face."

He spoke with such a note of sincerity in his voice that Rosie felt as if she were being hypnotised.

"And you saw me again?"

"Every time I had leave. I came back to England with one idea, and one idea only—to see you!"

"Why did you not introduce yourself to me?"

"How could I presume to do that?" he asked. "I had very little money. I could not even afford to send you flowers, certainly not the sort of flowers, I knew only too well, other men were sending you."

He sighed again before he went on:

"No, I merely sat in the stalls and felt my heart beating faster every time you appeared. I knew when I left London and you that I loved you even more than I had done previously."

"I can hardly believe it!" Rosie said. "But of course you are married?"

"I never found anyone who could even begin to equal you."

"I can only hope that you do not blame me for your remaining a bachelor!"

"You may not believe me, but it happens to be the truth," Stephen Hardcastle answered. "I love you, Rosie, so that I went to bed at night dreaming of you, and everything I did was with the object of making you proud of me."

Rosie still felt she could hardly believe what she was hearing.

Yet it was impossible to doubt that the man sitting beside her was telling the truth.

His voice vibrated with his love and she could see the sincerity in his eyes.

"Everything I did which gained the commendation of my superiors I did for you."

He paused before he went on:

"And when I finally inherited my ancestral home, I redecorated some of the rooms, thinking as I did so that they would be a perfect background for you."

He looked at her and his expression told her more than words that he was speaking from his heart as he said:

"And now that you are beside me, you are exactly as I thought you would be when you grew older!"

A smile lit up his eyes.

"From being a breathtakingly lovely young girl, looking at the world with starry eyes, you are now a distinguished and, of course, very beautiful woman."

"But you still did not try to meet me?"

"Perhaps I was afraid of being disillusioned," Stephen Hardcastle replied. "I had worshipped you for so long that you were enshrined in my heart as I had last seen you."

He gave a little laugh.

"I could not have borne it if you had been like so many older women with dyed hair, over-painted faces and looking, to put it bluntly, like 'mutton dressed as lamb.'"

He gave a laugh again, but this time of sheer happiness as he went on:

"But you are perfect, as I knew you would be, and I find it almost impossible to tell you how much that matters."

"I cannot believe it!" Rosie murmured.

Even as she spoke she knew she wanted to believe it.

They talked for an hour as they sipped champagne.

Then, when Stephen Hardcastle found that Rosie was going to be alone for luncheon, he called his valet.

They walked a little way from the Casino to the gardens of the Metropole Hotel.

"I am staying here," Stephen said, "because there are not so many steps as there are at the Hôtel de Paris, and also, I like eating in the sunshine."

"So do I," Rosie agreed.

She felt as she spoke there was sunshine in her heart.

Over luncheon Stephen told her how many times he had seen her at the Gaiety in the Shows in which she had appeared.

He made her understand how much it had hurt him when after a long time abroad he had gone eagerly to the Gaiety after she had left to find she was no longer in the cast.

"I could not imagine there could be a Show without you.

"Although it was an agony to lose you, I hoped very much that you were married and happy with someone who would look after you."

"There was . . . no one," Rosie said in a low voice.

"Oh, my dear, if only I had realised it!"

He put his hand over hers.

Then he asked, and she knew it was difficult for him to find the words:

"And now is there—someone in your life who—matters?"

Rosie told him the truth.

"There has been no one for a very long time."

She smiled at him.

"I came here only because my niece, whom I had never seen until a fortnight ago, came to me when her father and mother had died and she was alone."

Rosie thought of the years when she had sat doing nothing, seeing no one, merely living with her memories.

"There is no one," she said again, "and I left the stage when I was forty-five because, to be truthful, I was never an actress, only a Gaiety Girl."

Stephen drew in his breath, then asked, and she knew the question was very important:

"Do you—miss it all?"

"I often ask myself that question," Rosie replied. "I think what I miss more than anything else is the life I gave up when I went on the stage."

"Tell me about it."

As if his voice compelled her to do so, she found herself telling him about her girlhood, her family, and her father's fury when she had run away with Vivian Vaughan.

Only when she was telling him of how her life with Vivian ended did she realise that Stephen must never know what had occurred after he had left.

She did not want him to learn about the Marquis, and still less about the men who had followed him.

The one man she had prayed would marry her must not spoil the image Stephen had of her.

Because she knew how lightly a man would prize a woman he could buy, she was aware that she must not destroy the shrine he had made for her in his heart.

"So you suffered too, Rosie," he said gently as she finished speaking.

Then his fingers tightened on hers as he said:

"Is it possible that I can make it up to you?"

She looked at him enquiringly, then away again, and he said very quietly:

"I am proud of my home which is in Devonshire with its two-thousand acres of farmland, and of my position in the County."

He looked at her searchingly.

"At the same time, I am very lonely and you did say, Rosie, that you liked the country."

Rosie drew in her breath.

She could hardly believe what was happening, and yet, his hand on hers was strong and it made her feel as if already he was protecting and comforting her.

Then in a voice which did not sound like her own she said:

"You must . . . marry and have a . . . son to carry on . . . your title."

"That is not important," Stephen said, "because I have a nephew who has so distinguished himself in my Regiment that I am sure he will attain the rank of General with a Knighthood."

He paused, to continue proudly:

"I have another nephew who is in politics and may even achieve a Peerage."

His eyes were on Rosie's profile as he said very softly:

"That leaves only me, Rosie, if you will have me."

She turned to look at him, and for a moment she was no longer fifty-six but a young girl, shy and excited, because a man was in love with her.

"How can you say . . . all this to . . . me now," she said, "when you have only . . . just met . . . me?"

There was a touch of tears in her voice, but Stephen laughed and it was a very gentle sound.

"I have been trying to explain to you," he said, "that I have known you for so many years, and there is nothing you can say or do that will stop you belonging to me."

He stopped to smile at her before he continued:

"You are mine, Rosie, mine, in my mind, my heart, and my soul. The only thing you have to decide is whether you will come with me, or leave me to go on dreaming about you."

"Do . . . you . . . really want . . . me?"

It was the question of a girl who wants to be reassured, and Stephen said very simply:

"I will spend the rest of my life making you aware of how much."

*　*　*

There was a little Restaurant in La Turbie where the food was delicious.

Madame sat beaming attentively on the guests while her husband cooked in the kitchen.

Ina looked across the table at the Viscount.

They were sitting in the window, and because he had brought her up to La Turbie in his new car, she had taken off her hat.

She had tied a piece of chiffon over her hair.

It had been a very exciting drive for her since it was the first time she had ever been in a car.

The Viscount told her it was a racing Panhard which had the previous year been fitted with a new type of steering-wheel and pneumatic tyres.

Then they stopped outside the Restaurant.

Ina picked up her small straw hat which sat on the back of her head like a halo and gave her the look of an angel.

"Leave yourself as you are," the Viscount said. "There is nobody of any particular importance in this Restaurant, but the food is delicious and we can talk without being interrupted."

Ina thought it was only he who could be interrupted since she knew nobody in Monte Carlo.

Then she thought of the Grand Duke and gave a little shiver.

The Viscount must have read her thoughts because he said:

"There will be no one like that here, I assure you,

and as I have already said, it is a place where we can talk."

She smiled at him and put her hat back on the seat from where she had taken it.

She walked over the cobble-stones to the door of the Restaurant which, as the Viscount had said, was quite small and unimpressive.

He took a long time in ordering what they should eat, and when the food came, it was delicious.

Ina, however, was conscious only of his eyes on her and how handsome he looked against this quite different background.

She had no idea, because she was so un-self-conscious, that he was thinking the same of her.

Yet the expression in his eyes made her shy and she found it hard to look at him.

The waiter brought them wine, which the Viscount explained was grown locally.

When they had finished their luncheon and had been served with coffee and a glass of cognac, he said:

"I am worried that you were frightened this morning by the Grand Duke, and I want to make sure it is something that does not happen again."

"H-how can you do . . . that?" Ina asked.

Then she gave a little cry of fear as she went on:

"You do not suppose Aunt Rosamund will accept his invitation to stay at his Villa or visit his yacht?"

"I am sure your aunt will understand that you dislike him," the Viscount answered, "but I think it would be easier if you allowed me to protect you from the Grand Duke and all other men like him."

He paused before he went on very quietly:

"You are so beautiful, Ina, that you must understand that wherever you go, there will always be men who will find you irresistible and who will want to possess you for themselves."

"You are . . . frightening me!" Ina exclaimed. "I cannot believe there are many men as horrible and as . . . wicked as the . . . Grand Duke!"

"Why do you say that of him?" the Viscount asked. "What do you know about him except that he frightened you this morning?"

"I told Aunt Rosamund that you had come . . . upstairs with me . . . in case he should . . . approach me again . . . and she told me he was . . . married!"

The way Ina spoke, with a note of horror in her voice, told the Viscount all too clearly how innocent she was.

But he could not help suspecting that Rosie Rill's niece must have a better idea of the ways of the world than she appeared to have.

"Surely you understand," he said, "that when the Grand Duke and a lot of other men besides come to Monte Carlo, or go to Paris, they think they are free of the family obligations which would bind them in their own homes."

He paused before he said:

"Therefore they set out to enjoy themselves with any pretty girl they meet."

Ina gave him an incredulous glance before she said:

"It may be true . . . although it seems horrifying of . . . foreigners, but I cannot believe that Englishmen like . . . you would . . . behave in such . . . a way."

"Supposing," the Viscount said, "an Englishman like me saw a very beautiful, very lovely young woman whom he found irresistible and whom he could look after and protect? What would you expect him to do?"

Ina looked puzzled before she replied:

"I should have thought that was obvious. If he was unmarried, he would marry her, and if he was married, he would just have to forget her."

She spoke quite positively, as if she really could not conceive any alternative.

For the moment the Viscount was nonplussed.

He now realised that what he had been about to say to Ina would shock her profoundly.

Perhaps, if he expressed himself too hastily and too soon, she might run away from him as she had run away from the Grand Duke.

He therefore deliberately talked to her about La Turbie.

When he had paid for the luncheon they walked up to where the pillars were all that was left of what had once been a Roman Villa gleaming in the sunshine.

"If only they could talk!" Ina said. "What interesting things they could tell us."

"Are you really interested in history?" the Viscount asked.

He was thinking that few women he had ever known had shown any real interest in history, unless it concerned him or themselves.

"Papa and I used to travel all over the world in our minds," Ina replied. "We could not afford to go to Rome."

She smiled at him.

"But we visited the Palaces, the Churches, the fountains, and all the beautiful places that were created in it century after century in the same way that we visited Greece."

She went on after a moment:

"We were spellbound by its beauty, as thousands of pilgrims had been before it was desecrated."

She spoke with a rapt little note in her voice which told the Viscount how much it meant to her.

He drove her home, negotiating skilfully the twisting roads down to Monte Carlo.

He knew that he had not succeeded in explaining to Ina the part he wished to play in her life.

In fact, he was prepared to bet that she had not the slightest idea of what he had wanted to say to her.

He found it intriguing and fascinating that she was so different from every other woman he had ever known.

His father having set the example, he had, at an early age, taken a pretty Ballerina under his protection.

But she was so lacking in intelligence that he soon became bored, and she lasted barely six months.

He then turned to the Gaiety Girls, finding them glamorous and far more attractive than the performers in any other Theatre in London.

Quite a number had passed through his hands.

He had found them boring when what they said was always banal.

Also so predictable that he knew before they opened their pretty lips exactly what words would pass through them.

He found that Ina, young though she was, stimulated his mind because the questions she asked him were so intelligent.

He thought privately that he would have to "brush up" on his history and his general knowledge, unless he was to admit ignominiously that he did not know the answers.

They arrived back in Monte Carlo at about four o'clock.

As he drew up outside the Hôtel de Paris, the Viscount said:

"I shall see you this evening, for I am going to suggest to your aunt that I look after you while she gambles at the Casino, and perhaps we might go somewhere where I could dance with you."

"Dance with me!" Ina exclaimed. "That would be

absolutely thrilling! But . . . supposing I do not dance well . . . enough?"

"I do not anticipate that I shall be disappointed." The Viscount smiled. "Take care of yourself until then."

"Of course I will," Ina said, "and thank you very, very much for a lovely time. I have enjoyed myself more than I can possibly say."

"I am glad of that."

The Viscount looked into her eyes and had an almost desperate longing to kiss her lips.

Then as she ran up the steps into the Hôtel, he drove down to the Quay.

His father's yacht, *The Mermaid,* was in the harbour.

He thought he would suggest taking Ina and perhaps Rosie as well, if she wished to accompany them, for a cruise along the coast.

He parked his car and walked aboard to find the Captain waiting for him.

"Good-afternoon, M'Lord! I was hoping to see you."

"I thought I might take the yacht out tomorrow," the Viscount said.

He discussed with the Captain where they would go and ordered the food that would be required for a luncheon.

It would excel the excellent meal they had enjoyed today.

He thought how excited Ina would be at inspecting the yacht which had come from the shipbuilders only six months ago.

It contained every up-to-date gadget.

After they had talked for some time, the Captain said:

"If you'll come up on the bridge, M'Lord, I'd like you to look through the binoculars which you ordered in London and which arrived yesterday."

"Good!" the Viscount exclaimed. "I was just going to ask you if they had come."

They went up onto the bridge.

The Captain produced two pairs of binoculars which the Viscount had bought in London after he had been told they were more powerful than anything previously manufactured.

He picked up one pair and, lifting them to his eyes, looked out to sea.

Then up to the top of the mountain towering over the Principality.

He could see the Roman pillars that had excited Ina earlier in the day.

He thought of her interest and the questions she had asked him about the Roman occupation about which actually he knew very little.

He was thinking perhaps he should buy a really comprehensive history of Monte Carlo.

The Captain, who was looking through the other pair of binoculars at the crowds in the town, said:

"I can hardly believe it, M'Lord!"

"What is it?" the Viscount asked.

"I've just seen a young girl come out of the ravine. She must have been to the Chapel of Sainte Dévote."

The Captain looked concerned as he continued:

"I'm sure she was alone, but two men, who looked to me very like Russians from the *Tzaravitch* which is moored about three places from us, bundled her into a carriage. I'm sure she was trying to resist them."

"What are you talking about?" the Viscount asked sharply.

"Look, here comes the carriage driving down to the Quay," the Captain said, pointing to the roadway.

The Viscount followed the direction of the finger with which he was pointing.

He saw a closed carriage driving very quickly past them and move a little way down the harbour, where it came to a standstill.

The Captain beside him was looking and he said:

"I may be wrong, but I'm sure those two belong to the crew of the *Tzaravitch*, which is the Grand Duke Ivor's yacht."

The Viscount started.

Then again looking through the binoculars, he could see two seamen, both tall and overpowering, pulling Ina up the gangplank of the *Tzaravitch*.

There was no mistake it was her.

He thought, although he could not hear from this distance, that she was protesting.

Then, with an exclamation of anger, he put down the binoculars and started to leave the bridge.

He moved as quickly as he could.

But it took him the best part of a minute to reach the gang-plank leading down onto the quayside.

As he did so he looked toward the *Tzaravitch* and saw that it was already leaving its moorings and heading out to sea.

The Captain was just behind him and he said to him sharply:

"Follow as quickly as you can! I am going in the motor-boat!"

His motor-boat, which was a new acquisition like his car, was moored beside the yacht.

As the Viscount hurried towards it, two seamen on the Captain's orders followed him.

They started it up in record time.

"You come with me!" the Viscount said to one of them.

Then he set off to follow the *Tzaravitch*.

He heard the engines of *The Mermaid* and knew it would not be long before the yacht was at sea.

As he saw the spray from his motor-boat catch the beams of the setting sun, he told himself furiously that the Grand Duke would pay for this.

There was no doubt that Ina had been kidnapped.

"It is just the sort of thing that damned Russian would do," the Viscount told himself angrily.

The Grand Duke appeared to be suave, civilised, polished, and extremely well-mannered on the surface.

Yet not far underneath there was something primitive.

It made him, at times, behave in an outrageous manner which offended every accepted social convention.

The Viscount was furious now that he had not been more alarmed by Ina's fear of the Grand Duke.

He might have guessed that her running away from the Grand Duke would excite him.

He would be determined, however much she might try to evade him, to possess her.

The Grand Duke Ivor was notorious for his love affairs and they were too common an occurrence in Monte Carlo for anybody to be surprised.

But the Viscount knew that to Ina, who he was now convinced was as pure and innocent as she appeared to be, what was happening to her at this moment would be absolutely terrifying.

"I have to save her!" he murmured between gritted teeth.

His motor-boat had a Priestman engine which ran on kerosene, and a high-tension ignition.

He managed to make it achieve an even greater speed than its makers guaranteed.

Although the *Tzaravitch* was an older boat than *The Mermaid*, it, too, was built for speed and was already well ahead.

"Has my yacht yet left the harbour?" the Viscount shouted to the seaman above the roar of the engines.

"Yes, M'Lord, her's jus' a-comin' out."

The Viscount had no clear idea why he needed the yacht.

But he felt it offered some support and might give him a better chance of rescuing Ina than if he were just in a racing motor-boat.

But he went on, straining every nerve to increase his speed.

As eventually he caught up with the *Tzaravitch*, he wondered how he could get aboard.

Or at least in some way communicate with the Grand Duke.

Then suddenly he saw, and it seemed incredible, somebody dressed in white run across the deck.

For a moment the Viscount just stared.

He knew it was Ina, but he wondered how he could make her aware that it was he who was in the motor-boat.

Then as he watched her, at the same time man-oeuvring the motor-boat closer to the *Tzaravitch*, he saw her climb over the deck-rail.

She hovered for a moment, looking down at the sea.

Then as the Grand Duke appeared in a doorway behind her, she threw herself into the swirling water below.

chapter seven

WHEN the Viscount left Ina at the Hôtel de Paris, she had run quickly up the stairs.

She wanted to tell her aunt about her first drive in a motor-car and the beauty of La Turbie.

It was disappointing when she opened the door of the Sitting-Room to find it empty.

Then she realised that Rosie was not in her bedroom.

She was so longing to tell somebody of her experiences that she thought she might ring for Amy.

Then she had another idea.

Because she was happy and so grateful for everybody being so kind to her, she thought her first obligation should be to go to Church and thank God.

She did not think there was an English Church in Monte Carlo.

The Chapel of Sainte Dévote, however, was not far from the Hôtel.

She thought that if she ran down the hill to it,

perhaps by the time she got back her aunt would have returned.

She therefore retraced her steps, not going through the hall in case the Grand Duke should be there.

Instead, she left the Hôtel by a side door, which was used for luggage and for guests who were leaving with it.

Out in the sunshine she hurried quickly down the hill which led to the harbour, thinking that no one would notice her if she did not linger on the way.

She had no idea that the Grand Duke, who was leaving the Hôtel de Paris late after luncheon, was just behind her in a carriage.

She turned into the ravine and up the steps into the little Chapel, unaware that her every movement had been noticed.

The Chapel was very quiet.

There were only two women there, kneeling in prayer and waiting their turn to enter the confessional.

Ina walked to the other side of the Church and knelt down looking at the altar.

Shutting her eyes, she began to pray.

She made every effort to only give thanks, as her father would have instructed her to do.

Yet she found herself praying that the Viscount might feel a little for her what she felt for him—in fact that he might love her.

"Only a little . . . God," she prayed, "just a little because . . . I know he is too . . . wonderful for me to mean . . . anything in his life . . . but when we are . . . parted I want him to . . . remember me."

She prayed for what seemed to be a long time.

Then almost as if she felt she had received an answer to her prayers, she went from the Church and out into the ravine.

She was so intent on her thoughts that she did not notice there was anyone about.

Until, as she emerged onto the roadway, two men suddenly appeared one on each side of her.

She looked up at them at first in surprise, then in consternation, as one of them gesticulated towards a carriage, saying:

"*M'mselle* cum wi' us!"

He spoke with a strange accent, but Ina thought that he must be French and replied:

"No! I am going back to the Hôtel."

As she spoke, the two men, one on each side of her, caught hold of her arms and started to pull her towards the carriage.

She gave a cry of protest and struggled violently, but it was no use—they were too strong for her.

Almost before she realised what was happening, she had been pulled into the closed carriage and was sitting between them on the back seat.

"What are . . . you doing . . . where are you . . . taking me?" she asked in a frightened voice.

They did not answer, but only looked out of the windows towards the harbour where the yachts were moored.

"Y-you have . . . no right to do . . . this!" Ina insisted.

While she was still thinking of what else she could say, the carriage came to a standstill.

Opposite there was a large yacht with its gang-plank lowered onto the quayside.

One of the men got out of the carriage and started to pull her towards it.

She gave a cry of protest, saying: "No . . . no . . . you are . . . making a mistake!" but it was no use.

The other man helped to push her towards the gangplank and while she was struggling her hat fell off but neither of them would stop to retrieve it.

As one of them continued to pull and the other to push, they forced her up the gangplank and onto the yacht.

A few seconds later they opened the door of what she knew must be the Saloon and thrust her inside.

At first it was hard to focus her eyes.

Then, as she saw the Grand Duke Ivor rise from a sofa at the far end of the Saloon, she knew who had brought her here.

For a moment she was speechless.

"Welcome aboard, lovely lady," he said. "I have been waiting impatiently to talk to you and now at last we are alone."

Ina drew in her breath.

"How . . . dare you . . . bring me here . . . by force!"

She meant to speak angrily, but the Grand Duke was so tall and overpowering that her voice sounded breathless, young, and frightened.

He held out his hand.

"Come and sit down and I will tell you all about it."

"I . . . I cannot . . . stay," Ina insisted. "I have to go back to . . . Aunt Rosamund who is . . . expecting me."

The Grand Duke smiled before he said:

"I feel sure your aunt will understand when you tell her later why you were detained."

Ina crossed the Saloon towards him and looked up at him to say:

"Please understand . . . it was very . . . wrong of you to bring me here in such a . . . frightening manner."

She paused and caught her breath before she continued:

"Perhaps it was . . . wrong of me to go to the Chapel alone . . . but I wanted to . . . pray."

"And what were you praying for?" the Grand Duke asked. "I would be very interested to hear what you desire, so tell me what you want and I promise I will get it for you."

"What I . . . want is to . . . return to the Hôtel," Ina answered, "so . . . please . . . Your Royal Highness allow . . . me to . . . l-leave."

"There is no hurry," the Grand Duke said. "Let me give you a glass of champagne which will make you feel better."

"I . . . want . . . nothing!"

Ina put her hand up to her hair as she spoke and added:

"My hat fell off while . . . your men were . . . dragging me up the . . . gang-plank."

"I will give you another one, in fact, a thousand hats, if you want them."

He poured out two glasses of champagne and set one on a side-table beside Ina before he sat down beside her.

"Shall we drink a toast?" he said beguilingly. "To our happiness together!"

Ina stiffened.

"I . . . I do not know what . . . Your Royal Highness means. . . ."

She thought as she spoke that it would be a mistake to drink anything in case the wine should affect her in any way.

She therefore took only a tiny sip and put the glass down on the table beside her before she said:

"Please . . . Your Royal Highness . . . let us be . . . sensible. I have to go . . . back to Aunt Rosamund and . . . perhaps we can . . . meet another time."

She knew as she spoke that the last thing she wanted was to see the Grand Duke ever again.

She knew that somehow she had to get away from the yacht.

But she was sure if she tried to escape, his servants would prevent her from doing so.

The Grand Duke drank half a glass of champagne before he, too, put his glass down.

Then he reached out and took Ina's hand in his.

Her fingers were stiff and unyielding, but he did not seem to notice as he said:

"You are very lovely: in fact, more beautiful than anyone I have seen for years!"

He had a leer on his face as he continued:

"What I am going to do, Ina, is to give you everything in the world you want—gowns, jewels, furs, a carriage, horses, and when we leave Monte Carlo, a house in Paris where we will be very happy."

For a moment Ina stared at him in sheer astonishment, then she said:

"I cannot . . . understand why Your Royal Highness . . . should wish to do anything . . . so extraordinary, and I understand you have . . . a wife in Russia who would be . . . I am sure . . . very glad of such . . . things."

"My wife has everything she needs," the Grand Duke replied, "but because you are so beautiful, my little Ina, you need the right sort of frame to portray your beauty."

"It is quite . . . impossible for me to . . . accept any of the . . . things you have suggested."

Ina spoke in a small voice as she went on:

"In fact . . . although I must . . . thank Your Royal Highness for your . . . generosity I can only . . . refuse your offer and now . . . I must go!"

She jumped to her feet as she spoke.

She would have turned towards the door if the Grand Duke had not put out his hand to catch her by the wrist.

He held her captive.

Then, as she struggled ineffectually to free herself, he very slowly rose to his feet.

"There is no escape," he said very softly. "I want you, and because I intend to conquer you and to make you love me, it is even more exciting than if, like most women, you were complaisant."

The way he spoke in his deep voice with the trace of an accent made a streak of terror run through Ina like forked lightning.

She had thought he was menacing when he first spoke to her, but now she knew he was terrifying and utterly repulsive.

She was very innocent, at the same time she knew that what the Grand Duke was suggesting was wicked.

The mere idea of his touching her gave her a feeling of horror that made her want to scream and go on screaming.

Now he was pulling her towards him, determinedly and slowly, as if he savoured the idea of holding her captive.

She struggled and twisted and fought to be free.

Relentless, he drew her nearer and nearer until his other arm went around her and she felt herself imprisoned as if with steel bands.

She tried frantically to push him away.

She knew as he gave a low laugh deep in his throat that he was not only amused, but excited by her resistance.

"Let . . . me go! Let me . . . go!" she cried.

As she twisted her head from side to side to try to prevent him from kissing her, she felt his mouth, unable to capture her lips, hard and insistent on her neck.

Then, as she still struggled, his teeth bit the softness of her skin!

For a moment she was frozen with terror into immobility.

Then she felt his hand on her breast, seeming to sear her body through the thin silk of her gown, like an animal's paw.

"We will go to my cabin," the Grand Duke said. "I want to hold you close to me, closer than we can be here, and I will teach you about love, which I find very exciting!"

There was a deep, passionate note in his voice which to Ina sounded like the growl of a savage animal.

With his arm around her, the Grand Duke was forcing her towards the door, and she felt despairingly like a victim and a slave.

But she would rather die than let him do what he intended.

He moved quickly, as if he were in a hurry, and she realised she was terrified by him.

She was also so appalled that she knew that if, as he threatened, he made her his, then she would no longer wish to go on living.

All this flashed through her mind while she was too frightened to think coherently.

The Grand Duke opened the door of the Saloon.

She began to pray desperately to her father, to Sainte Dévote, and also to the Viscount.

It was almost as if she could see his handsome face looking at her, and it was then she knew that only he could save her.

"Save ... me! Save ... me! Oh ... God ... let him ... save me!" she prayed in her heart.

In one split-second the opportunity was there.

The Grand Duke relaxed his hold so that they could pass through the door.

With a strength she did not know she possessed, Ina fought herself free.

She slipped away from him and rushed through the door that led out onto the deck.

She ran across it wildly, reached the deck-rails and climbed up them.

Holding on to a bar which was part of the frame-work of the awning, she looked down into the sea.

She knew that if she threw herself overboard, she would die, since she could not swim.

Then behind her she heard the Grand Duke call out:

"Come here, Ina, you little fool!"

Without hesitating another second, she threw her-self into the water below.

As she did so the Viscount stood up in his motor-boat, pulled off his coat, kicked off his shoes, and dived into the sea.

The seaman with him immediately took his place at the wheel.

He directed the boat as the Viscount swam with strong strokes towards the place where Ina had dis-appeared.

He guessed that as she had simply thrown herself into the sea, probably she could not swim.

Any way she would have been knocked out with the violence with which she had hit the water.

She came to the surface only a few feet ahead of him.

As he caught hold of her he was aware that she was unconscious.

As he supported her he heard shouts from the deck of the yacht which had by now been carried by its own impetus farther on.

He paid no attention, ignoring a life belt that had been thrown overboard.

Holding Ina's head above the water, he swam with strong kicks of his legs toward the motor-boat.

Because she was so small and light, it was easier than it would have been with anyone larger.

Or indeed with anyone who was conscious and perhaps panicking.

As he held her up, the seaman lifted her into the motor-boat.

Then as he clambered aboard himself he could hear the Grand Duke bellowing angrily at him from the *Tzaravitch*.

Ignoring him, the Viscount swung the motor-boat round and set off towards *The Mermaid*, which was still some distance away.

As he did so he looked back and saw that a life-boat was being lowered from the *Tzaravitch*.

He knew, however, it was very unlikely that it had an engine in it.

In any case, his motor-boat was faster than anything that had yet been seen in Monte Carlo.

When they reached *The Mermaid*, Ina was still unconscious, but she was deftly lifted aboard and the Viscount followed.

He carried Ina down to the Master Cabin and the Captain, who was skilled in First Aid, followed.

Having put Ina down on the floor, the Viscount went into the bathroom to pull off his wet clothing.

Wearing a Turkish-towelling gown, he came back into the cabin to find a large pile of towels had been put beside Ina.

The Captain rose from her side to say:

"She's still unconscious, M'Lord, but I think it is just from shock and the violence with which the young lady hit the water. Her pulse is steady."

"I will get her into bed," the Viscount said, "then perhaps you could look at her again."

"I'll do that, M'Lord. Do you wish us to sail back to Monte Carlo?"

The Viscount thought for a moment, then he said:

"No, tell the seaman in the motor-boat that I have a letter for him to deliver which I will write in a few minutes. Until I have done so—cruise slowly back along the coast."

"Very good, M'Lord."

As the Captain left the cabin the Viscount knelt down at Ina's side.

She looked, he thought, with her hair wet and her gown clinging tightly to her figure, like a nymph who had risen from the sea.

With experienced hands he undressed her, thinking as he did so that it was the first time he had ever undressed a woman who was completely unconscious.

He tried not to think of how beautiful she was and that her body was like that of a Greek goddess.

As swiftly as he could he wrapped her in the towels.

Then, having laid others on the bed and one on the pillow, he lifted her up very gently and laid her on them.

Only then did he allow himself to look at her for a long moment, realising that her eye-lashes were dark against her pale cheeks.

With her lips drooping a little, as if she were unhappy, she was so lovely that he wanted more than he had ever wanted anything in his life to kiss her back to consciousness.

Resolutely, however, he pulled a sheet over her and, going to the door, said to the Captain:

"Your patient is ready for you, Captain. I will just go above and write a letter I want taken to Monte Carlo."

"Very good, M'Lord. I'll stay with the young lady until you return, but I don't think she'll wake."

The Viscount did not answer, but hurried up the Companion-way and into the Saloon, where there was a writing-desk.

He sat down, and taking a piece of thick vellum writing-paper engraved with the yacht's name, he wrote:

Dear Lady Rosamund,

Ina was abducted by the Grand Duke Ivor and taken away on his yacht the Tzaravitch. She escaped by throwing herself into the sea from which I have rescued her.

She seems to be unhurt but is still unconscious, and I am taking her to Villefranche to stay with my Great-Aunt, the Duchess of Wrexham, who has a Villa near there and a trained Nurse always in attendance.

I will call on you tomorrow morning to let you know how Ina is, and discuss her future.

Yours sincerely,
Victor Colt.

He put the letter into an envelope and addressed it to Lady Rosamund at the Hôtel de Paris.

He told the steward to give it to the seaman on the motor-boat with instructions to deliver it as quickly as possible.

He then returned to his cabin and told the Captain to proceed to Villefranche with all possible speed.

The Viscount then dressed himself, and sat down beside the bed to look at Ina.

It took nearly two hours before they entered the harbour of Villefranche.

The Viscount sent a seaman ashore to notify his aunt that he was coming to stay and bringing a visitor with him who was at the moment in ill health.

He also asked her to send her carriage to convey himself and Ina to the Villa.

It was after eight o'clock when finally the Viscount was informed that the carriage was at the quayside.

A quarter-of-an-hour later he carried Ina ashore and laid her very gently on the back seat of the carriage.

The elderly Nurse sat opposite her, but she did not move on the drive which carried them by way of the Upper Corniche Road to the Duchess's Villa.

Now the sun had set and the stars were coming out in the sky.

The Viscount was, however, concerned only with Ina and the fact that she looked very frail.

On their arrival at the Villa he carried her up the stairs to where a bedroom had been prepared for her.

"Do you think Miss Wescott will be all right?" he asked the Nurse, who had been with his aunt for some years.

"She's young and the young are very resilient, M'Lord," the Nurse answered. "I don't think you've any need to worry."

After he had laid Ina down on the bed, the Viscount went to find his aunt.

She was an old lady and partially immobilised, and had lived alone for the last eight years.

"This is a surprise, Victor!" she said, holding out her hands as he entered her bedroom.

The Duchess had once been a great beauty, but since her husband's death she had never been in good health.

She found it boring to take second place to the new Duchess, who had supplanted her when her son inherited the title.

She had therefore retired to the South of France, where a large number of English people lived.

She reigned, as the Viscount had told her mockingly, "like a Queen."

He bent towards her and kissed first her hand, then her cheek, before he sat down beside her and told her what had happened to Ina.

"I have never heard anything so disgraceful!" the Duchess exclaimed. "But all the Grand Dukes, because they are Royal and rich, think they rule the

144

world and ordinary conventions do not apply to them."

"I would like to call him out," the Viscount said savagely, "but I think it would be a mistake to cause a scandal."

"If you did that, you would ruin the wretched girl's reputation for ever!" the Duchess said. "Apparently you have saved her, or rather, she saved herself, and now the best thing you can both do is to forget it!"

"I quite agree with you, Aunt Alice," the Viscount answered, "and, as you are always very wise, I shall follow your instructions."

The Duchess laughed.

"I very much doubt that! You have always had your own way, Victor, which is very bad for you. But like all the other silly women in your life, because you are so handsome, I find you irresistible!"

The Viscount laughed.

Then as he was told dinner would be ready for him in half-an-hour, he went to his bedroom to bathe and change into his evening-clothes.

*   *   *

Ina felt as if she were moving down a long, dark tunnel and there was just the faintest glimmer of light at the end of it.

With what was almost a superhuman effort she opened her eyes.

Then as a man moved towards her she remembered the Grand Duke and gave a little scream of terror.

As her lips moved, it was only just audible as she said beneath her breath:

"Save . . . me! Oh . . . God . . . save me!"

"He has saved you!" a deep voice replied. "You are safe now, Ina, completely and absolutely safe, and it will never happen again."

It was the voice she had longed to hear and was very comforting.

Ina turned her head like a child to press her cheek against his hand.

Then the voice came again:

"You are safe. Go to sleep and I promise no one shall hurt you."

She tried to move a little closer, then as she slipped away back into the darkness of the tunnel she thought she felt something touch her forehead very gently.

It sent a little thrill through her body.

* * *

"Well, you certainly look better this morning!" the Nurse said as Ina sat up in bed, her fair hair falling over her shoulders.

"I am well, of course I am well!" Ina replied. "Can I get up?"

"If the Doctor says you can. He's coming at eleven o'clock."

"Please tell him how good I have been, taking all his medicines and eating, even though I did not feel hungry."

"You had better tell him yourself," the Nurse replied, "and I have a feeling he'll let you have luncheon on the balcony with His Lordship."

She saw Ina's eyes light up and it was as if a thousand candles were behind them.

She told herself as she left the room that this beautiful girl was in love with a man who, judging by his reputation, would in all likelihood break her heart.

She sighed as she walked down the corridor, knowing there was nothing she could do about it.

* * *

The Viscount had seen Ina for only a brief moment the previous afternoon.

It was after he had returned from Monte Carlo, having visited Rosie.

He told Rosie what had happened and she had exclaimed angrily:

"How dare the Grand Duke behave in such an outrageous manner!"

The Viscount had not replied and after a moment she had looked at him and said:

"I suppose it was my fault, and was what one might have expected when the girl in question is the niece of Rosie Rill!"

The Viscount paused before he said quietly:

"That is something I want to talk to you about."

"Let me tell you something first," Rosie said. "Incredibly, for I never expected such a thing to happen, I have promised to become the wife of a man who has loved me for many years, although we never met until now."

The Viscount looked incredulous as she went on:

"His name is Sir Stephen Hardcastle, and as he has never enjoyed the Social World, we are going to live in Devonshire where he has an Estate."

She paused before she said:

"I am praying that 'Rosie Rill' can be forgotten except by him. That is the best thing that could happen so far as Ina is concerned."

The Viscount smiled.

"That is something I was hoping to talk to you about, but now there is no reason for me to do so."

"None at all," Rosie said. "I knew what you intended when you took her to stay with your Great-Aunt."

She gave a sigh before continuing:

"Although I shall always love Ina because she is one of the sweetest people I have ever met, it would be best if we did not meet again—at least—not for a long time."

"I agree with you," the Viscount said, "and I think, Rosie, no one could retire with more grace and dignity."

"'Lady Rosamund' to you, in the future!" Rosie said teasingly, "and mind you do not forget it!"

The Viscount kissed her hand.

Amy was told to pack all Ina's clothes, and he informed Rosie he had ordered a brake to call for her trunks during the afternoon.

He then drove off in his Panhard car to see his father.

He expected he would have to face an uncomfortable encounter with Lady Constance.

It was a relief to find that she was not in the Villa, but had gone into Monte Carlo with Lord Charles.

It was therefore far easier to make explanations not face to face, which would doubtless have led to recriminations.

Instead, he wrote her a long letter which he hoped made everything clear.

It also meant that he could be alone with his father.

When he returned to his aunt's Villa it was to find Ina had been awake for a short time, but was very tired.

The doctor was pleased with her, however, and said that although she had a slight concussion, it was nothing very much to worry about.

All she had to do now was rest and not be in a hurry to do anything strenuous.

Darkness had come with its usual swiftness as the Viscount dined alone.

He was content to do so because his brain was busy with his plans for the future.

Ina came out onto the balcony, where he was waiting for her the next day.

With her hair arranged simply in a *chignon* at the back of her head she looked very lovely.

Also so young and innocent that she might indeed be the Greek goddess the Viscount had thought her to be as he undressed her on the yacht.

Now she was wearing one of the beautiful and expensive gowns from Bond Street which her aunt had bought her.

It did not detract from the childlike innocence and aura of purity which enveloped her.

It would have been impossible for anyone not to know how happy she was to see him.

As her fingers clung to his, the Viscount could feel her vibrating towards him as he knew he vibrated towards her.

"You are better?" he asked.

"I am well . . . thank you," she replied, "but I have been given 'strict instructions' to behave like an invalid. However, because I am so happy to be here and . . . safe, I want to . . . dance on the clouds . . . or run down to the sea!"

Then because she was afraid he would think her over-dramatic, she said:

"How can you have been so . . . kind to bring me to this . . . lovely place? And the Duchess has been very . . . very sweet . . . to me."

The Viscount did not speak, he only looked at her and Ina went on a little shyly:

"B-but first . . . I must thank you for . . . saving me. I prayed that you . . . would do so . . . but I never thought you would . . . really be there . . . and I expected to . . . die."

The Viscount drew her to the sofa which had been arranged on the balcony beside a table on which they were to have luncheon.

They were shaded by a large blind from the rays of the sun.

Yet the warmth of it seemed to Ina to seep into her whole body as the Viscount, having taken her hand in his, did not release it.

"I want you to forget what happened with the Grand Duke," he said quietly. "It was something that should never have taken place and I swear to you will never occur again."

"I think . . . you told me I was . . . safe when I . . . was unconscious," she said in a hesitating little voice. "I knew then I was . . . alive and that . . . you were there . . . and nothing else . . . mattered."

"Nothing does matter!" the Viscount said firmly. "And now, Ina, we have a great deal to talk about, and I have a lot to tell you."

He paused before he continued:

"But because I have been given strict instructions that you should not be tired, I suggest we have our luncheon first."

She gave him a quick glance.

He knew she was apprehensive as to what he was about to say.

As the servants brought out the dishes the Viscount insisted on her having a glass of wine.

He made her laugh by his stories of the excitement caused by his Panhard car, and the difficulties he had experienced two years ago when he had driven one for the first time.

Time seemed to fly by on wings.

Then the servants moved the table and they were alone.

Once again the Viscount drew Ina to the sofa.

"I wanted to ask you if Aunt Rosamund is . . . all right," Ina said, "and is not . . . angry with me for staying . . . here with . . . you."

"I have seen your aunt," the Viscount replied, "and I have some news which I know will delight you."

Ina waited, her eyes on his, and he went on:

"Your aunt is to be married to Sir Stephen Hardcastle who, it seems, has loved her for many years!"

"Married?" Ina exclaimed. "But I never imagined I . . . never thought of Aunt Rosamund marrying again . . . but of course . . . it is a wonderful idea! Now she will no longer be lonely . . . or miss the Gaiety Theatre."

"I agree with that," the Viscount said, "and your aunt thought you would understand that, as they wish to be married at once."

"At once?" Ina exclaimed.

"She will be leaving Monte Carlo with Sir Stephen," the Viscount continued, "and they are going to live in Devonshire, where he has a large house and an Estate."

Ina drew in her breath, then she faltered:

"D-did . . . Aunt Rosamund . . . suggest what . . . I should do?"

"I told her what I suggested," the Viscount replied, "and she thought it a very good idea."

He paused, then Ina said as if she could not help herself:

"Please . . . I do not want to go back . . . to Monte Carlo. I . . . might meet the . . . Grand Duke . . . or other men . . . like him. Could you . . . arrange for me to . . . go to England?"

"I agree with you that Monte Carlo is not right for you," the Viscount answered, "and I intend to take you to England eventually, but I have thought of something to do first which I hope will interest you."

Ina looked puzzled, then she said in a nervous little voice:

"I . . . I have already told you . . . that I have very few . . . talents for . . . earning money."

The Viscount smiled.

"I remember," he said, "but there will be no need for you to do that."

He saw Ina stiffen.

Reading her thoughts, he knew she imagined he was going to offer her money and was determined to refuse it.

"What I want to ask you," he said very quietly, "is what you feel about me."

Her eyes widened as he went on:

"I know you have been frightened by the Grand Duke and I think the sort of men you will meet in this part of the world will also frighten you."

"Of course . . . they will," Ina said, "but . . . I have always felt . . . safe with . . . you."

She turned her head away before she said in a different voice:

"I realise I . . . must not be an . . . encumbrance on you . . . but I would rather take . . . your advice than anybody . . . else's. It is very . . . very difficult to know what I can do or where I can go . . . without getting . . . into trouble."

She gave a little shiver as she spoke.

The Viscount knew that once again she was thinking of the Grand Duke.

"Forget him!" he said. "As I have told you before, I will look after you."

"I have tried to . . . thank you for that," Ina replied, "but . . . when you . . . leave me. . . ."

"Who said I was going to leave you?"

She looked at him as if she did not understand, and he said:

"What I am suggesting, Ina, is that you stay with me, not just for a short time, but for the rest of your life."

For a moment her eyes were filled with stars and he thought that no woman could look more radiant, more happy.

Then, as she thought she was dreaming, she looked out towards the sea and said:

"I . . . I do not . . . understand what you are . . . suggesting."

The fear was back in her voice as she was thinking of the Grand Duke's offer of clothes, jewels, horses, and a house.

"What I am suggesting," the Viscount said very softly, "is that you should marry me—that is—if you love me!"

Ina gave a little gasp.

Then as her fingers tightened on his, as if she must make quite certain he was real, she said:

"Are you . . . really asking me . . . to m-marry you?"

"I cannot see how otherwise I can look after you."

"It . . . it cannot be . . . true!"

The words were only a whisper, and yet he heard them.

"It is true, my darling."

Very gently he put his arms around her and drew her close to him before he said:

"And this is true too. I have never, my precious, ever asked any woman to marry me before, and I have never wanted a wife until I found you."

"Are you . . . sure . . . absolutely sure that I am the right . . . person for you?"

Before he could answer she went on:

"I love you . . . of course I love . . . you! I love you until there is . . . nothing and . . . nobody in the world but you . . . but then, I have . . . lived very quietly and

153

seen very . . . few people."

She paused before she continued:

"You are so grand . . . you could m-marry any of the beautiful Ladies who . . . I am sure . . . love you just . . . as I do."

"I do not think that is true," the Viscount contradicted. "The way we love each other, Ina, is very different from what the 'beautiful Ladies' as you term them, in Monte Carlo and in London feel for me or for any other man."

"Why is it . . . different?"

"Because, my darling, I think I knew from the first moment I saw you that we were made for each other."

As he spoke he knew that Ina must never be aware of what he was intending to offer her when he took her to luncheon at La Turbie.

It was not only because she was Rosie Rill's niece that he was prepared to give her what was called his "protection."

It was also because he was fighting a losing battle against giving up his independence.

His freedom to pass from flower to flower, throwing away those which faded or else no longer attracted him.

But Ina, as he had been aware from the first moment they met, drew him like a magnet.

He had found it impossible not to think of her every moment of the day and during the long stretches of the night when he could not sleep.

When he saw her throw herself into the sea he had known that he could not lose her.

If he did he would lose something so precious, so wonderful, that he would be crippled for the rest of his life.

He would be like a man without an arm or a leg, although in his case, it would be without his heart.

He knew now that he wanted nothing more than to protect Ina, take care of her, and have her always with him.

Everything had been made remarkably easy.

First because Rosie was to be married.

She would step out of the picture and cease to be an embarrassment, although Ina was not aware of it.

What was more, once she was his wife, his friends and relatives would accept her.

He was sure no one would remember she was Rosie's niece or that her mother had married a poor parson.

She would be accepted as the granddaughter of the Earl of Ormond and Staverley.

Also as the Viscountess Colt and later the Marchioness of Colthaust, the Ormonds would be delighted to welcome her.

As far as he himself was concerned, none of them mattered; he was marrying Ina because he loved her.

But it would make it easier for her, and that was important.

Also, when yesterday the Viscount had lunched with his father, the Marquis had told him that the doctors in Monte Carlo had warned him against returning to England.

"They tell me my heart is in a 'dicky' state," he said, "and my lungs are not particularly strong."

He had laughed before he added:

"I expect it is the result of a lifetime of riotous living, although I do not regret any of it."

"I am sorry, Father," the Viscount had said in all sincerity.

"I knew you would be, my boy," the Marquis replied, "but what I have decided will affect you."

"In what way?"

"I intend to stay here in the Spring and Summer, but go farther South in the winter, following the sun, which is preferable in every way to the cold and un-predictability of the weather in England."

He smiled before he finished:

"I doubt if I shall make 'old bones.' So I shall enjoy myself in my own way and certainly not give up anything I find amusing whether it is good for me or not!"

The Viscount smiled, knowing that as his father was still a very good-looking man, there would also be attractive women in his life.

"What I want you to do," the Marquis continued, "is to take over Colt Park and all my other estates and run them, I am sure, far better and more efficiently than I have been able to do."

He paused.

"In fact, as you well know, I have never given enough time to them. There is a great deal to be done, and also, I should hate to think of my horses not being entered for the Classic Races. I certainly want to hear from you every time they win."

For a moment the Viscount was silent, then he had said:

"You know, Father, I will keep you informed and do everything I can to keep everything going as it should."

"I expect you will need a wife to help you," the Marquis remarked. "I could not have managed as well as I did without the help of your mother."

"That is just what I was going to tell you," the Viscount replied.

Now, as he held Ina against him, he knew that just as he could help her, she would be able to help him.

When they talked together, she stimulated his mind.

She also aroused everything that was noble and chivalrous in his nature.

It was difficult for him to explain, even to himself, how different she was.

The women he had known had always been ready to take everything they could extort from him.

But, when he looked back, apart from their bodies, they had given him very little else.

He knew now that something within him responded to Ina's purity.

He was inspired by what he could describe only as her "holiness" in a way he had never expected.

He desired her as a woman because she was so beautiful that it was impossible for him not to do so.

But to him she was already a shining star illuminating the way and he would follow her to the end of his life.

Now, as his arms drew her closer to him, he knew that she was trembling.

Yet it was not with fear, but with an excitement that was echoed within himself.

Very gently he turned her face up to his.

Then, as he looked down at her, her eyes looking at him shyly, her lips quivering a little, he said:

"I have dreamt of this!"

His lips held hers captive and his kiss was at first gentle and tender.

Then as it became possessive and demanding, he knew it was different from any other kiss he had ever been given by a woman.

With Ina, it came not only from her heart but her soul.

It was so intense and so rapturous that it was an ecstasy that seemed to lift them up into the sky.

"I . . . love you . . ." Ina whispered. "I love you but . . . I still . . . cannot believe that you . . . really love me."

"It will take me a long time to convince you," the

Viscount answered, "and that is why, my darling, I thought for our honeymoon we would go away on *The Mermaid.*"

He smiled at her before continuing:

"We will explore exciting places which you told me you have visited in your mind with your father, but now you will visit in reality with me!"

"Can we . . . do that?"

"We will go to Greece, then on to Turkey, and through the Suez Canal to the Red Sea."

Ina gave a cry of joy and he went on:

"There is so much of the world I want to show you, and I think, my precious, we shall be living in a world of our own; a world of love, where nobody will disturb us."

"I am dreaming . . . I know I am . . . dreaming!" Ina whispered. "Please . . . kiss me . . . again before I wake . . . up."

The Viscount gave a little laugh and it was a very tender sound.

Then he was kissing her, not as gently as he had done before, but demandingly.

It was as if he must make quite certain she was his and no one would ever take her from him.

Only when they were both breathless did she hide her face against his shoulder, and the Viscount said tenderly:

"I have already arranged our marriage. It is easy because, as my father has a house in Paris, I count as a resident in France, and there will be none of the delays there would be in England."

As he spoke, he knew it would not matter to Ina or to him where they were married as long as they were husband and wife.

* * *

Two days later, they said good-bye to the Duchess, who was overjoyed at their marriage.

When they stepped aboard *The Mermaid,* Ina was like an excited child.

"It is such a lovely little ship!" she cried.

"That is what I wanted you to say," the Viscount replied. "Although it was my father's, he has given it to us as a wedding-present because I supervised the building of it and installed all the very latest gadgets which I am longing to show you."

"And I want to see them."

She looked very lovely as she spoke.

She was wearing an elaborate white evening dress that had been amongst the other gowns which Rosie had bought for her.

Covering her head was a magnificent lace veil which the Duchess had worn at her own wedding.

She had also given Ina a tiara as a present, saying when she would have protested:

"I have no further use for it, my dear, and as I wore it when I was married, and I was very, very happy, I feel it will bring you luck."

"How could I be luckier than be able to . . . marry such a wonderful . . . marvellous man?" Ina asked.

The rapture in her voice was very moving.

The Duchess looked at her nephew.

She realised that he had changed a great deal since he had fallen in love with this lovely, unspoilt child.

She had been saddened in the past by the cynicism she had heard in his voice.

She had hated the mocking twist to his lips when he was talking to some beautiful woman.

But she knew that now there was sincerity about him that was very different from what she had seen before.

"They will be happy," she said to her Nurse as they left the Villa.

* * *

As the Viscount showed Ina over *The Mermaid*, he knew he had never known such happiness.

When the yacht moved out of Villefranche harbour into the open sea, he took Ina below.

They went into the cabin, which she had never seen, but where she had been taken after he had rescued her from the sea.

Now it was massed with flowers: lilies, roses, gladioli, and orchids.

All of them had been bought fresh that morning in the Flower Market in Nice.

"How can you have bought all these for me?" she asked.

"If I could, I would have bought you the sun, the moon, and the stars, and given them to you too!"

Then as she looked at the flowers with delight he added:

"The last thing my great-aunt and her Nurse said to me was that I must take care of you and see that you had plenty of rest."

He smiled very tenderly as he went on:

"That is why, my darling, I am going to make you rest now. It is quite a long time before we have dinner."

Ina gave a little cry of protest.

"I . . . do not want you to . . . leave me!"

The Viscount smiled.

"There is no question of my doing that."

She understood and blushed.

"I did not . . . think . . . " she began.

"My precious, my perfect little wife," he said, "I have so much to teach you about love. I promise I will be very gentle, but I want you, and I feel that I have waited centuries to have you in my arms, and make you mine."

She gave a little laugh of sheer happiness.

Then as he lifted the tiara from her head, took away the veil, and undid the back of her gown, she said:

"Y-you are . . . making me feel . . . shy."

"This is not the first time I have undressed you."

She looked at him wide-eyed and he explained:

"When I rescued you from the sea, I put you first into my motor-boat, then I carried you into this cabin and laid you on the floor because you were dripping wet."

"I must . . . have looked . . . terrible!"

"I thought you were like a nymph from the sea, but when I took off your wet clothes I knew you were not a nymph but a goddess from Olympus!"

Now the colour flooded into Ina's face and as her gown fell to the ground she moved a little closer to him, saying:

"Please . . . do not look at me again . . . in case you are . . . disappointed."

"How could I be disappointed with anything so beautiful that even the flowers pay you homage because they know you are even more perfect than they are."

"How . . . can you . . . think . . . that?"

"I will tell you what I think and what I feel," the Viscount replied.

He lifted her up in his arms as he spoke and carried her to the bed.

Then as she lay looking at the flowers as they filled the air with their fragrance, he joined her.

The yacht was moving smoothly through the calmness of the sea.

But as the Viscount put his arms around Ina and drew her to him, he knew his heart was behaving tempestuously and he loved her passionately.

At the same time, because he loved her, he was frightened of hurting her or making her afraid.

He knew from his long experience that he had to

be controlled and very gentle.

He kissed her forehead, her eyes, her little straight nose, then the softness of her neck.

Her lips were parted and ready for his kiss, but he kissed her breasts until she quivered against him, then lastly her mouth.

When he kissed her and felt a little flicker of flame respond to the fire burning in him, he knew they were on the threshold of the ecstasy of perfect love.

A love that was so pure and so holy that nothing harsh or ugly must ever spoil it.

It was the beauty of the flowers, the sun, the stars, and the moon.

The beauty that came from God and which was goodness itself.

It had nothing to do with the wickedness and the perversions of mankind.

"I love . . . you," Ina whispered. "How can . . . I thank God for letting . . . me find you and that . . . you love . . . me."

"I love, adore, and worship you," the Viscount said hoarsely.

"You are so wonderful . . . so very . . . very . . . wonderful."

There was a touch of passion in her voice that she did not understand, but the Viscount replied:

"You are . . . mine . . . all mine forever."

Then as he and Ina became not two people but one, he knew that their love would protect them.

It would keep them safe from all that was wrong and evil.

It was a love, he knew, that would last not only throughout their lives in this world, but into eternity.

There, by the mercy of God, they would still be together.

ABOUT THE AUTHOR

Barbara Cartland, the world's most famous romantic novelist, who is also an historian, playwright, lecturer, political speaker and television personality, has now written over 450 books and sold over 400 million books the world over.

She has also had many historical works published and has written four autobiographies as well as the biographies of her mother and that of her brother, Ronald Cartland, who was the first Member of Parliament to be killed in the last war. This book has a preface by Sir Winston Churchill and has just been republished with an introduction by Sir Arthur Bryant.

Love at the Helm, a novel written with the help and inspiration of the late Admiral of the Fleet, the Earl Mountbatten of Burma, is being sold for the Mountbatten Memorial Trust.

Miss Cartland in 1978 sang an Album of Love Songs with the Royal Philharmonic Orchestra.

In 1976 by writing twenty-one books, she broke the world record and has continued for the following ten years with twenty-four, twenty, twenty-three, twenty-four, twenty-four, twenty-five, twenty-three, twenty-six, and twenty-two. She is in the *Guinness Book of Records* as the best-selling author in the world.

She is unique in that she was one and two in the Dalton List of Best Sellers, and one week had four books in the top twenty.

In private life Barbara Cartland, who is a Dame of the Order of St. John of Jerusalem, Chairman of the St. John Council in Hertfordshire and Deputy President of the St. John Ambulance Brigade, has also fought for better conditions and salaries for Midwives and Nurses.

Barbara Cartland is deeply interested in Vitamin Therapy and is President of the British National Association for Health. Her book *The Magic of Honey* has sold throughout the world and is translated into many languages. Her designs "Decorating with Love" are being sold all over the U.S.A., and the National Home Fashions League named her in 1981, "Woman of Achievement."

In 1984 she received at Kennedy Airport America's Bishop Wright Air Industry Award for her contribution to the development of aviation; in 1931 she and two R.A.F. Officers thought of, and carried, the first aeroplane-towed glider air-mail.

Barbara Cartland's Romances (a book of cartoons) has been published in Great Britain and the U.S.A., as well as a cookery book, *The Romance of Food,* and *Getting Older, Growing Younger*. She has recently written a children's pop-up picture book, entitled *Princess to the Rescue*.

BARBARA CARTLAND

Called after her own
beloved Camfield Place,
each Camfield novel of love
by Barbara Cartland
is a thrilling, never-before published
love story by the greatest romance
writer of all time.

More romance from

BARBARA CARTLAND

Available at your local bookstore or return this form to:

JOVE
THE BERKLEY PUBLISHING GROUP, Dept. B
390 Murray Hill Parkway, East Rutherford, NJ 07073

Please send me the titles checked above. I enclose _____. Include $1.00 for postage and handling if one book is ordered; add 25¢ per book for two or more not to exceed $1.75. CA, NJ, NY and PA residents please add sales tax. Prices subject to change without notice and may be higher in Canada. Do not send cash.

NAME_____

ADDRESS_____

CITY_____STATE/ZIP_____

(Allow six weeks for delivery.)